DESIGNS FOR MARKETING

NUMBER ONE

DESIGNS
NUMBER ONE
FOR MARKETING

PRIMO ANGELI

ROCKPORT PUBLISHERS
Rockport, Massachusetts

Distributed to the book trade and art trade in the
U.S. and Canada by:
  North Light, an imprint of Writer's Digest Books
  1507 Dana Avenue
  Cincinnati, OH 45207
  Telephone: (513)984-0717

Distributed to the book trade and art trade
throughout the rest of the world by:
  Hearst Books International
  105 Madison Avenue
  New York, NY 10016
  Telephone: (212)481-0355

Other distribution by:
  Rockport Publishers
  5 Smith Street
  Rockport, MA 01966
  Telephone: (617)546-9590
  Telex: 5106019284
  FAX: (617)546-7141

Copyright © 1988 by Rockport Publishers Inc. All rights reserved. No part of this book may be reproduced in any form whatsoever without the express written permission of the copyright owner, Rockport Publishers Inc., 5 Smith Street, Rockport, Massachusetts 01966

Designs For Marketing Number One was produced and prepared by Blount & Company, Number 12 Station Road, Cranbury, New Jersey 08512

Library of Congress Cataloging in Publication Data:
  Designs For Marketing

  Includes Index

  1. Primo Angeli
  2. Graphic Design - international

ISBN 0-935603-07   87-060502

Book design by Jamie Davison Design Inc.,
San Francisco, California

Printed and bound by Mandarin Offset,
Hong Kong

Designs For Marketing Number One was composed and typeset on an Apple Macintosh II publishing system. The type was output via Allied Linotronic 300 by Graphic Connexions Inc., Cranbury, New Jersey.

PRINTED IN HONG KONG

10 9 8 7 6 5 4 3 2 1

Editors:
Steve Blount
Lisa Walker

Designers:
Jamie Davison
Kent Tayenaka

Project Coordinator:
Terry Sellards

Art Assistants:
Philippe Becker
Carl Feryok
Jeffrey Schaefer
David Teich

Photographers:
Henrik Kam
Ming Louie
Lars Speyer
John Vano
Tom Vano

Administrative Assistant:
Irene Weisser

Dedicated to Deanie Angeli

CONTENTS

Foreword   9
    by Dick Coyne, Editor & Designer,
    Communication Arts magazine

Introduction   10
    by Kevin Starr, Professor of
    Communication Arts and American
    Studies, University of San Francisco

Twelve Stories

Blitz-Weinhard	16
Lucca Delicatessens	24
Christian Brothers	28
TreeSweet	34
Conoco	42
Boudin & Toscana Breads	46
DHL Corporation	52
Shaklee	56
California Coolers	62
Capri Sun	70
Asian Art Museum	74
Cambridge Diet Formula	80

Gallery

Package Designs	86-107
Trademarks and Logotypes	108-119
Signage, Brochures, Identity Programs	120-125
Posters	127-136

Inside Primo Angeli Incorporated   138

FOREWORD

In 1959 a handsome young man in his mid-twenties arrived in San Francisco to seek a career in design. The date is easy to remember because it was precisely the time my design firm was launching *Communication Arts* magazine. Since then, I have watched Primo Angeli's career develop. In fact, he has designed three *Communication Arts* covers, has been featured twice in articles and has judged one of our Design Annuals.

It may sound as if the path to an international reputation was easy. It wasn't. Primo had received a solid education in design theory with a Bachelor of Arts and Masters degrees from Southern Illinois University, during the time that Buckminster Fuller was on campus, not to mention visiting resident designers of the caliber of Will Burton and Aaron Burns. But when he arrived in San Francisco, a city that perennially attracted more talent than jobs were available, Primo's experimental student portfolio couldn't get him a position.

Realizing his shortcomings, he went to work for a small, but innovative, litho shop in Palo Alto, California, where he learned the practical side of design and production. This stint at freelancing was followed by a partnership with illustrator Dick Cole. He finally opened his own design firm in San Francisco in 1967.

Primo Angeli describes his firm's work as "marketing design," a saleable term for problem-solving by close interaction with the client's marketing department. This approach to design solutions may have prohibited him from developing a strong personal style, but his ability to combine appropriateness with esthetic quality has won him his share of design awards. His more personal expression is reflected in his product development and numerous poster designs, often pro bono publico for worthwhile causes.

Dick Coyne, Editor & Designer,
Communication Arts magazine

INTRODUCTION

This is a book about the theory and practice of graphics communications. It brings theory and practice together by analyzing process. Process is the bridge between theory and practice. The American philosopher William James described the relationship between theory and practice as pragmatism. He also believed that pragmatism was a quintessentially American attitude. Americans, James observed, never fully knew what they were doing—in terms of theory, that is—until they actually embarked upon the process of doing it. This book chronicles a number of competitive, pragmatic encounters with the process of graphics communications at the Primo Angeli Inc. studio in San Francisco, California.

The Primo Angeli style, however, is empowered by more than its pragmatic American inspiration. Primo Angeli completed his graduate work at Southern Illinois University in the late 1950s under such Bauhaus-inspired mentors as Buckminster Fuller, Harold Cohen and Herbert Roan. During these years, Angeli absorbed a design philosophy that can best be summarized by Maholy Nagy's statement: "Design is not a profession but an attitude." Nagy, the man largely responsible for bringing the Bauhaus to the United States, viewed design as a total, encompassing, service-oriented approach based upon the ability to listen, to observe, to analyze and to serve—and not merely to impose doctrine and solution upon a client.

As practiced at Primo Angeli Inc., competitive graphic communications constitute an existential, market-oriented blend of esthetics, communications and salesmanship. Pure esthetics has its place; but what would pure esthetics mean to a client whose business had been ruined because an esthetics solution turned out to be a marketing disaster? If money provides the engine power of the graphics design ship, marketing criteria provide the keel and the rudder. Who, in other words, is a client trying to reach and with what message? Answering this question involves establishing the range of visual reference, the level of taste, the span of attention, the degree of sophistication and other conditionings of the audience which directly affect the modes of visual symbolism that can be most effectively absorbed. Each product has a target audience, or a cluster of target audiences; and in seeking to conjoin product, audience and visual symbol, marketing and design draw upon sociology, psychology and anthropology.

Thus, each of the design solutions chronicled in this book represent complex social and psychological statements. Perceived in their ongoing activity as communication symbols, they are fluid, still in process, like language itself. The argument can be made, in fact, that graphic communication is an emergent visual language that one day might achieve an analyzable grammar, syntax and vocabulary. For the time being, such suggestions might remain speculative; yet in experiencing the design process as narrated in this intriguing book, one constantly encounters the steps by which an appropriate visual vocabulary and syntax are achieved experimentally, but with seemingly universalized results, as in the case of language.

Language is the basis of all human culture. Why should this not be true of visual language as well? Perceived as achieved probes into the mind and imagination of a targeted audience, the design solutions featured in this book can be considered cultural artifacts of major significance. Graphic symbols are, after all, important components of the modern urban environment. Sometime in the early twentieth century (was it with Sunkist oranges, Dutch Girl cleanser, Camel cigarettes, Jello, Kleenex, Hershey chocolate bars, Carnation Evaporated Milk?), trademarks and logos began to emerge as persistent icons of identity. Not only did visual symbols package and communicate a specific product, they became in and of themselves fixed elements of visual reference, poised on market shelves like gargoyles or statuary in a medieval cathedral. Not only did such logos, trademarks and product designations become synonymous with the product—Kodak, Kleenex, LifeSavers, Coca-Cola, Jello, Xerox—they also achieved significance as social and psychological reference points. Why, for example, is it necessary each decade to update such icons as Betty Crocker, Aunt Jemima, Uncle Ben and others? Why have other packaging solutions—Camel cigarettes and Hershey chocolate—remained constant? In each instance, the icon in question has achieved solidity as a fixed visual symbol. Like a Jungian archetype, these emblems stores, preserve and recycle social and psychological experience. To survey the history of American trademarks is to encounter a succession of cultural probes and barometers. Trademarks of the 1920s, for instance, frequently present visual evidence of the transition from a rural/agricultural economy to an urban/industrial society. Trademarks from the Great Depression are rich in escapist imagery and streamlined articulations of experience that contain within themselves the promise of flight, fantasy and escape. Decoding the implication of past and present trademark symbols and packaging solutions remains a nascent art; yet their pervasive power is attested by their sheer survivability. Is it because, in part, such visual symbols provide each of us with reference points on our own journey to identity? In a world of constant change, that is, certain packaging solutions appear and reappear decade after decade with a comforting message of stability amidst the ever-changing process. Is it because every successful visual package contains a valuable social message, a form of tribal totem for modern urban society?

Whatever the answers to these questions, a number of the packaging solutions achieved by Primo Angeli Inc. will make the roll call of enduring icons. Indeed, Angeli's solutions for Henry Weinhard beer, Boudin Sourdough bread, Molinari & Sons salami, Just Desserts, Christian Brothers wines and Banana Republic are already considered classics.

Not surprisingly, Primo Angeli delights in the poster as an art form. A number of posters emanating from Primo Angeli Inc.—The Silent Majority, now in the permanent collection of the Metropolitan Museum in New York City, being the most conspicuous—have already made the transition from graphics communication to fine art. The poster is the prototype of all modern graphics communication. Europeans have been especially sensitive to the poster as fine art. In the 1960s, at a time of social stress, this awareness of the poster as fused social communication and fine art came to the United States with great force. The Silent Majority survives as one of the dozen or more powerful posters of this era. As competitive graphics, to use Primo Angeli's favorite term, it communicates. It also stores and represents experience with moral meaning and great symbolic power.

Like everything else issuing from the studio of Primo Angeli Inc., this book is part of an ongoing process. This book is about a continuing journey as well as about destinations which have been achieved. Angeli and his colleagues remain convinced that graphics must never become imprisoned in one style, even if that style has brought success. In today's rapidly evolving society, the avant grade can soon become the obsolete. It is only by continuous anticipation of the future that classics can be achieved. That is the paradox of competitive graphics communication. Its heritage resides in its futurity and its futurity is its heritage. From this perspective, it is no accident that Primo Angeli established and developed his studio in California, given the special sensitivity of this region to the process whereby the future is anticipated and invented. Nor is it irrelevant that a number of current projects at Primo Angeli Inc. deal with products and programs emanating from the Pacific Rim, toward which the futurity of the United States is tending.

Some thirty-five years ago, Primo Angeli, then an undergraduate, encountered what has proved to be one of the most influential books of his career, "Zen and the Art of Archery" (1953) by Eugen Herrigel. From this book, Angeli absorbed an important lesson: The best way to get to the target is to aim at it and become one with it, all in one motion. There is a tendency in the West to break things down, to sort them out, to analyze them. But the East tells us, Zen tells us, not to become victims of our own methodology, to let the target determine the solution. The Zen of Primo Angeli Inc. is to seek to become one with the target, to move toward those moments of harmony and understanding in which the true solution, the lasting solution, is discovered. As much as it is a business, competitive graphics consulting is also an art form; and as such, it must remain subconscious, intuitive, as well as on budget and on schedule.

The art, finally, of the solutions suggested in this book constitutes its most enduring source of delight. Seeking the pragmatic, competitive solution, the designers of Primo Angeli Inc., like the patient disciples of the Zen master, have become one with the object of their design intention; and the result is at once competitive and beautiful.

Kevin Starr, Professor of
Communication Arts and
American Studies, University
of San Francisco

The Bauhaus was my school of design. For some of us it eventually translated into design for marketing and communication. I wish to acknowledge those special influences, both personal and distant, that continue to support this evolutionary visual art experience: Lars Speyer, Saul Bass, Herb Roan, Richard Cole, Milton Glaser, Harold Alldis, Harold Cohen, Hal Riney, Herb Meyer, Dick Coyne, John Crane, Theodore Pashedag, Maholy Nagy, Walter Landor, Paul Rand, Yusaku Kamekura and R. Buckminster Fuller.

TWELVE STORIES

Fortune and circumstance sometimes contribute as much to success or failure as a clever strategy. When Blitz-Weinhard commissioned a package for a new superpremium beer, they got both. By unintentionally recreating a hundred-year-old logo, a way was opened to win an assignment and to inspire the loyalty of beer drinkers.

In 1975, Anheuser-Busch decided to greatly expand sales of its top-selling Budweiser beer in the Pacific Northwest. For the brewers of regional beers, such as Blitz-Weinhard of Portland, Oregon, it was clearly a case of the irresistible force—the giant St. Louis brewery—meeting some very removable objects. Blitz-Weinhard was concerned that the marketing muscle wielded by Budweiser meant their sales charts would soon look like they'd been kicked by a Clydesdale.

Blitz-Weinhard's only product was a popular-priced beer, which meant it was directly in the path of the St. Louis steamroller. The brewery had three options: meet Budweiser head-on and probably be obliterated in the process; create a new product that wouldn't compete directly with Budweiser; or punt—sell the company or close it down. They chose to go head-to-head with Anheuser-Busch, and began work on a superpremium beer that would be made in small batches using a 19th century brewing process. They also chose not to go it alone. Blitz-Weinhard called in Hal Riney, the San Francisco advertising maven.

I got a call from Hal Riney asking if I wanted to design the packaging for a new product. He knew my work for Boudin Bread, and thought that I would be able to create a solution for Blitz-Weinhard because of my experience not only with packaging, but with logotypes. He wanted to be able to lift the brand mark from the beer packaging and use it separately. When we met, Hal handed me a concise design brief. One of the great things about working with Hal is that he's always very clear about what the assignment is. He also dropped two bombshells. First, the start-up budget was small. Second, another designer was also working on the job. At some point, the client would decide which of us would be awarded the assignment.

The brewery was founded in 1856 by Henry Weinhard, a brewmaster who carted a 15-gallon copper vat from Germany to Oregon. The packaging had to reflect the hand-crafted methods he had used in order to convince drinkers that this was a beer of unusual quality.

There were four of us working in the studio at that time. One of my associates, Mark Jones, helped develop a number of comps, most using the Henry Weinhard name. The neck labels bore a unique batch number to

Our original comps presented to Hal Riney featured an eagle and two banners.

After the comps had been submitted, the brewery found this logo on a hundred-year-old tasting glass. Its similarity to our comps, especially the stylized initials entwined around the eagle, is eery.

In the comp for the final design, we replaced the eagle with a more stylized rendering, simplified the H and W and reworked the filigree surrounding the banners.

In the six months after we got the commission, our design team explored a number of alternatives. The client still hadn't decided what to call the product, so the wording on our comps varied as we wrestled with the name. We decided to use "Henry Weinhard" fairly early, but the legend "Private Reserve" wasn't added until much later.

make the beer appear special.

Most of the comps also carried a fair amount of copy talking up the brewery's history. Besides being informative, the copy made the product more believable. Even though it was new, we wanted the beer to look like it had been out for a while. When a consumer saw it, we didn't want them to say, 'Here's a new brand of beer.' We wanted them to think, 'Why didn't I see this beer before?' That reaction helps win acceptance for a new brand.

As a final "disaster check" focus groups were conducted. Participants favored dark green as a background color, which was reserved for future line extensions.

Our design team experimented with a huge number of designs and colors for the neck band.

The package had to project quality and tradition, but that wasn't easy to do. When you do a traditional product, it has to fit comfortably into a contemporary environment. That makes it comfortable for the consumer. "Ye Olde Fashioned" was not what we were going for. The brand mark caught people off guard because it was entirely conjured up for the moment, yet it carried some of the architecture of the past in the design. Weinhard wasn't a contemporary looking beer, but it *was* made for contemporary people.

When Hal saw the comps, he favored the ones that featured an eagle in the center. I had applied the brand mark to seven or eight different types of bottles and to a wooden beer case. Hal let me make the presentation, and after an hour or so of discussion, it looked rather like everyone was pleased with the results. Hal decided to recommend our design.

I went home that weekend feeling pretty good. We'd spent more time on the comps than we were likely to get paid for, but since I thought we had the job, I was

TWELVE STORIES 21

pleased. Hal called me on Sunday and said the presentation hadn't gone well. What a shock! Even though Hal preferred our work, Blitz-Weinhard wanted to use the other designer. Hal said he would try to turn them around and promised to call me the next day.

When Hal got to the studio Monday afternoon, he came with some very good news and an amazing artifact.

He told me he'd gotten Blitz-Weinhard to change their minds. I asked him what happened. He said, "This is what happened."

Hal reached into his coat pocket and pulled out an antique beer tasting glass inscribed with a logo: An eagle in the center with the words "Henry Weinhard" in a banner above and a bit of filigree to each side.

I was stunned. The symbol on the glass was so close to our comps

that only a reincarnation of Henry Weinhard in Hal or myself could have made this happen. It was so convincing because it was a link to Weinhard's history. We got the assignment partly by tapping into that historical source. It was one of those happy coincidences.

Blitz-Weinhard asked us to incorporate the logo from the glass with our comps and move on to a finished design.

Henry Weinhard Private Reserve was rolled out without fanfare—and without advertising. Hal's strategy was to have Private Reserve appear in very select bars—special watering holes that fit the superpremium image of the beer—to become a kind of discovered item. When the print and television ads broke later, the beer already had a base of loyal customers. The plan worked beautifully. A decade later, Weinhard is the number two superpremium beer in the Pacific Northwest and has been introduced in thirteen western states.

After the successful roll-out of Private Reserve, Blitz-Weinhard released the beer in cans and then began offering dark and light varieties. We did the packaging for these brand extensions as well.

It's hard to design tradition into a new product. Very often it looks contrived—it's too easy to be a victim of pretense or status rather than being believable.

Our label for Weinhard dark, introduced in 1983, won a gold in the Western Art Directors show in 1984. Weinhard Light came along in 1986. Its label won a Clio in 1987.

You need an accurate sense of the consumer you're designing for. If you can really put yourself in their shoes, then it's like designing for yourself. But you'll never succeed if you have a strong style that you must impart to every project. What's more, not knowing the target makes it an accident if you ever do arrive at a viable solution. Unfortunately, your failure will come at the expense of your client.

An ethnic name is a powerful plus when you're selling homemade pasta in delicatessens and supermarkets. But when that name is so common that it fills several pages of a metropolitan phone book, it's probably time to find some other way to distinguish your product. For Lucca Delicatessens, which sells an array of packaged pasta and sauces in the Bay Area, the solution was a five-letter ULTRA LUCCA *word.*

Lucca Delicatessens Inc. has been a part of the Bay Area landscape since 1948. When Paul Ferrari and his cousin Larry Cerlette bought the three-store operation from relatives in the early 1980s, they had ambitious plans to franchise the delicatessens and expand distribution of the stores' frozen pasta products into supermarkets. In 1983 they asked us to create a contemporary brand identity and packaging system for the Lucca line of frozen foods.

TWELVE STORIES

Lucca had been using the same graphics since 1948. Paul felt it was time to modernize the chain's image to match the quality of its foods and services. Paul admired our work for Molinari Salami and Boudin Bakeries, but he was looking for something less ornate; a look that would build equity for the Lucca name in a contemporary form.

As we worked, I began to wonder about the uniqueness of the name "Lucca." There are a number of businesses, including a famous chain of delis, called Lucca in the Bay Area. Paul wasn't worried. He felt that if the design was very strong, it would be enough to fully identify his establishments. After many experiments, we found a strong graphic system that did the job.

Several months after the new design was incorporated into the stores' signage, it became clear that consumers were confusing Lucca delis with other businesses, especially the Lucca Packing Company, which also produces packaged ravioli, tortellini and sauces. Paul reached back into the company's history and found that it had once been called "Ultra Lucca." We added "Ultra" to the design, which was just the touch needed to establish a clear identity.

We worked with a number of typefaces and geometric shapes to highlight the name. Red, green and white position the products as authentic Italian fare, while the white background conveys freshness. And the stencil typeface makes a bold statement in a crowded upright freezer or coffin case, and helps distinguish these Lucca products from others bearing the same name.

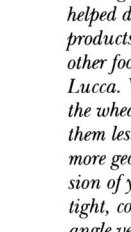

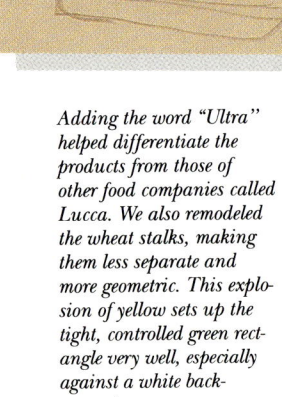

Adding the word "Ultra" helped differentiate the products from those of other food companies called Lucca. We also remodeled the wheat stalks, making them less separate and more geometric. This explosion of yellow sets up the tight, controlled green rectangle very well, especially against a white background.

We felt we could give these products an edge by creating a strong identity. If you pick up three oranges at random, they all look pretty similar at first. But when you look more closely, you find there are subtle differences. As a designer, it's crucial to appreciate these differences in order to communicate what's special about the product. Once that uniqueness has been found, the graphics should express it clearly.

The stencil typeface worked for these products in part because it has a handmade appearance. We used it to say that the Lucca products were handmade from family recipes.

Since its introduction on the covers of metal foil heat-and-serve trays, the design has been adapted for use on a variety of boxes and packages.

For more than 100 years, the Brothers of the Christian Schools have cultivated a successful wine-making business in California's infamous Napa Valley. Among the vast array of California wines, The Christian Brothers vintages have performed well. In 1983, the Brothers sought a new identity that would position them among the leaders in the growing varietal segment.

In 1879 The Christian Brothers, a lay religious teaching order of the Roman Catholic Church, opened a training school in Martinez, California, on property blessed with twelve acres of vineyards. It wasn't long before the Brothers began producing wine for sacramental purposes. News of the winery's quality vintages spread to the secular community and, by 1887, the Brothers found themselves firmly planted in the wine business.

T W E L V E   S T O R I E S

The business climate in the Napa Valley has changed considerably since the region's early wine growing days in the late nineteenth century. News of the region's fertile soil and warm, sunny climate has attracted legions of new winemakers. The competition heated up and so did consumption of California wines.

As American wine consumers became more sophisticated, their tastes increasingly turned away from generic wines—basic reds and whites—and consumption of varietals increased. In the early 1980s, The Christian Brothers winery found itself in a unique position. While sales of some of its bread-and-butter wines—generics and aperitifs—were down, its vintage-dated varietals were garnering one award after another. The time seemed right for The Christian Brothers to strengthen its flagship brands and to launch a series of premium varietal wines.

After 100 successful years, it's normal to be apprehensive about major changes. But there's a time-honored cure for such queasiness: market research. The Brothers were concerned that the order's religious association prejudiced drinkers against their products. They even considered launching their premium varietals under the name "Greystone." While that would have avoided the religious issue, it would also have prevented the winery from transferring the considerable equity of its existing line to the new varietals.

Instead, a marketing study found that very few consumers

The winery, established in Martinez, California, in 1887, later moved to the lush Napa Valley. It has since acquired properties in the San Joaquin Valley.

Market research revealed that consumers were impressed by the order's history as vintners, and by the winery's Napa Valley heritage—two elements that were retained from the original wine labels.

were put off by the name "Christian Brothers." In fact, it showed that the winery's Napa Valley location and century-long history were a plus, and that one in five consumers felt positive about the fact that the wine was produced by a religious order.

With this research in hand, the Brothers called us in to redesign the labels for the dessert and generic wines and to create a labeling scheme for the new varietals.

The Brothers were looking for a new identity, one that would position their premium varietal wines on the same plane as market leaders Paul Masson, Beringer,

For the premium varietals, we tried a number of designs using bands of rich colors. But ultimately we decided to forego the bands in order to focus more attention on the product name.

Almaden and Robert Mondavi.

When you're hired to update the image of an established winery, there isn't a lot of opportunity to explore new styles, avant garde typefaces and outrageous color schemes. You have to exercise a great deal of restraint. To be sure, some California winemakers have projected an ultra-contemporary image. But they're the exception.

We chose an uncoated, slightly textured paper for the varietals to give them a handmade look.

Most winemakers proudly display family crests and drawings of their wineries or vineyards on labels.

Our first step was to refine the marketing objectives. Mark Jones, Ray Honda and I presented the first series of black-and-white comps. We showed scores of different configurations for the label, focusing on the positioning of the name Christian Brothers. We spent an unusual amount of time creating rough sketches. But there were several major questions that needed to be answered: How much of the winery's heritage should be depicted on the label? What percentage of consumers immediately associate the current label—shaped like a chapel door—with Christian Brothers wines? How much tradition should we eliminate on the new labels?

After intense experimentation, we found a solution: The Christian Brothers name was reversed white against a rich, deep-colored band at the top of the label and accented with gold foil rules. A small rendering of the winery suggests the product's heritage. With the basic design scheme decided on, we

attacked with vigor the labels for the various classes of Christian Brother wines. First, the generics. Given the competition on the retail shelf in this category, it was important that the labels "read" quickly; we wanted consumers to be able to tell the variety of the wine in a glance. With this in mind, we positioned the product name in the center of the label. The white background, which was used in all of the designs, maximizes shelf impact.

A similar graphic treatment was created for the dessert wines, except that we chose an off-white background color for the ports and a cream-color backdrop for the sherries.

The dessert wines also carried a band, but the labels were printed on a glossy paper. This helped bring the image in line with the price point and taste level of the intended consumer.

Consumers take more care selecting varietal wines, so we created a slightly different label for them by stacking the words "The Christian Brothers" to make the name more prominent. The look is similar to that achieved using a letterpress, befitting their status as more expensive wines.

Some names are so euphonious, so magical, that they are almost—but not quite—the only thing a marketer needs to succeed. TreeSweet is one of those special names. When the business was acquired in 1984, we were asked to translate a great name into a powerful new identity. Married to an expanded line of products, the redesigned package helped TreeSweet crack new markets and increase distribution.

TreeSweet Products didn't have a lot going for it when it was acquired in 1984 by a management team led by veteran beverage marketer Clint Owens. The company's market position, driven by price, was quickly eroding. But Owens saw potential: For one thing, TreeSweet had a million dollar name. Names as colorful as "TreeSweet" aren't available; they're already taken. He knew it could encompass many products besides the orange juice it had been coined for.

There's no doubt that when you go to dance with the debutantes, you'd best wear a tuxedo. Clint Owens, the chairman of TreeSweet, already knew that when a group of private investors he headed bought TreeSweet from the DiGiorgio Corporation of San Francisco and moved it to Houston. Clint had been instrumental in doubling sales of Minute Maid juice products during his tenure at Coca-Cola Foods. He wanted to use TreeSweet to go after the market held by his former employers and by Beatrice Company's Tropicana and Procter & Gamble's Citrus Hill brand. Clint knew TreeSweet needed not just a face-lift, but a new image compatible with his Texas-size ambitions for the brand.

TreeSweet was an innovator in the frozen juice field through the 1960s. But by the time of the sale in 1984, it was competing on price alone in regional markets covering just a quarter of the United States.

Although this package had done well for the company, it was time for a change.

  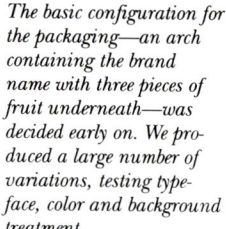

The basic configuration for the packaging—an arch containing the brand name with three pieces of fruit underneath—was decided early on. We produced a large number of variations, testing typeface, color and background treatment.

When we flew to Houston for the initial interview in February 1985 we didn't know how extensive the assignment would be. We assumed TreeSweet wanted new packaging for the orange juice. They did. But they also planned to introduce new products. Clint was determined to turn TreeSweet into a national competitor, and he wanted packaging strong enough to literally knock his competitors off the store shelves.

We made our presentation directly to Clint and several members of his marketing staff. I was in one of my more animated moods, very excited about the name and what we could do with it. Clint asked about naturalness, taste appeal and strong shelf impact. I told him we felt we could design a well-integrated package. Because the name was so long—nine letters—we had developed some diagrams to determine how to present the name, in a circle, over an arch or just on a straight line. We

To differentiate the various products within the line, we initially tried varying the treatment of the brand mark. While it looked good and the client liked it, we were afraid we'd run out of colors before finishing the line.

We adopted the strategy of changing the background of the labels to differentiate between the products. By keeping color changes to a minimum, the products create a much stronger billboard effect when shelved together.

Very thin vertical stripes, almost like a design from Victorian wallpaper, were added to give the package a feeling of richness and old-fashioned heritage.

showed them the diagrams and described how they might work on the cylindrical juice cans.

We got the assignment and immediately immersed ourselves in developing the concepts we had shown Clint. We all agreed that the arch was the best configuration for the name. We wanted the package to say "homespun" and "down to earth" to project the idea that these were the finest natural juices. The existing packaging was very 1950s, but it did have one interesting element: three orange spheres with smiling faces. The three spheres were redesigned and placed under the arch containing the name. Using those elements we produced countless variations and rolled them onto juice cans.

Clint deserves a lot of credit for encouraging the uninhibited exchange of ideas between our designers and his marketing people. Everyone was open to constructive criticism and nobody let their egos get in the way of a good marketing and design solution.

Over the next six months, with further refinements, the arch-and-spheres became very rich and natural looking. It fit comfortably on different forms of packaging while delivering impact and taste appeal.

Everyone was happy with the design, but with the deadline for the roll-out closing in on us, I became concerned that the serifs of the type we'd designed were a bit heavy. The heaviness caused the type to look a little old-fashioned. We slimmed the serifs and made them very sharp, more like the pointed serifs in Benguiat type. It looked cleaner and more contemporary immediately.

Just one element was missing. I suggested to Clint that, with all of the changes being made to the packaging, it might be a good idea to add the word "original" to reassure consumers that this was the same TreeSweet juice they had trusted for years. By placing "original" atop the arch just above the name, we created another point of interest.

We still had to decide how to distinguish the products in the line from each other. We explored changing the color of the band holding the TreeSweet name for each variety. Seeing the color changes on the range of products was beautiful and Clint liked it. However, given the range of products TreeSweet had planned, there was a danger we'd run out of colors before the company ran out of its new products. Also, I'm in favor of keeping color variations between varieties to a minimum. When the items are shelved together in the supermarket they create a strong billboard effect. We decided that the brand mark worked best as white letters in a blue band and that the background color of the packages would change for each item. Finally, we were satisfied that the label looked almost edible. The line was unveiled at a convention in December 1985.

Soon after, sales began to

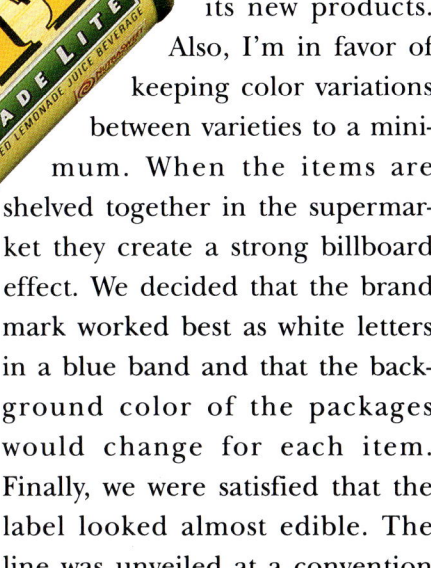

Even before the new TreeSweet packaging had hit the market, we were already at work on the company's first line extension: TreeSweet Lite.

shoot up; within a year, TreeSweet's market share rose from two percent to three percent.

As we completed these products, we began designing packages for a line of reduced calorie juices called TreeSweet Lite, which

debuted nationally the following spring. Although the designs were well-accepted, consumers apparently weren't ready for light juices. By year's end, sales of TreeSweet Lite were lower than the company had hoped. By mid-1987, market share of the full-calorie juices had slid back to two percent, exacerbating a chain of circumstances that led to a restructuring of the corporation.

TreeSweet Lite was the first reduced-calorie juice to be distributed nationwide. Our designs had to work on a wide variety of containers, and they had to be strong enough to win shelf placements for this brand new category in the hypercompetitive supermarket arena.

The challenge was to create a package that would visually fulfill the promises implied by the name TreeSweet: Fresh, natural, delicious fruit juice. Messages reach the tastebuds in both verbal *and* non-verbal ways. Non-verbal messages that evoke feelings and sensations can be very powerful. If you can say a product tastes good without using words, you're home. If you feel you want to take a bite of the product, wrapper and all, you've really done something.

Being the best and letting customers know you're the best are often two different things. Especially if, like Conoco, you're up against the likes of Exxon and Mobil. With their huge advertising budgets, the multinationals can bury the voice of a regional company like Conoco, making it hard to get the message of quality across to consumers. In order to strengthen Conoco's retail identity, we were asked to create new packaging that would reflect the quality of its products and give them more punch on the shelves.

How would you like to play in a basketball game where the other players were a foot taller than you? In a way, that's the situation faced by many regional companies like Conoco. Although its products are among the best on the market—they are the sole suppliers of Ford's Motorcraft lubricants—they were being outshouted by the big media bucks plunked down by Havoline, Pennzoil and the gasoline retailers.

TWELVE STORIES

Conoco has been a significant regional force in the oil industry for most of this century. But due to a unique gasoline distribution system—its retailers are allowed to carry any brand of products they wish—it has no dedicated outlets for its lubricants as do Mobil and Standard Oil. Nor does it have the media clout wielded by Havoline and Quaker State.

Knowing it was squaring off at a disadvantage, the company undertook a revitalization of its corporate identity and signage in 1987. At the same time, it asked us to redesign the packaging for about thirty products. Our mission was purely mercenary: Create packages that could go toe-to-toe with the national brands both within the Conoco service stations and in the environment of discount and auto parts stores.

Another key disadvantage was that Conoco does not discount its products as deeply as the national brands. Its volume is lower. And the company refuses to lower its standard of quality to knock a few cents off per quart.

Steve Barnhill, vice president of Brown & Barnhill, Conoco's adver-

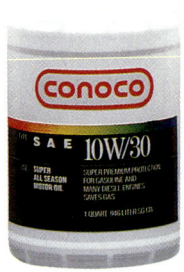

We created a number of full comps to demonstrate some of our design concepts. Although the company had been using gold containers, we recommended they switch to black.

tising agency and J.D. Haas, Conoco's director of merchandising, wanted the package to become a "powerful engine" in the company's marketing, rather than the "caboose" it had been, as they put it.

While we explored all the options, we decided early on that the packages would be black. Conoco's competitors were using predominantly white, yellow and gold containers. Black has a lustrous, look. And it is entirely consistent with the basic product, motor oil.

The new system was implemented for the motor oil and we've started adapting the new design to the company's other products.

A hang tag was created for the neck of the one-quart bottles to strengthen the impression of quality. It also gives the marketers another small but influential way to communicate with consumers.

Particularly for a client with a limited advertising budget, a good package can become a great equalizer. Advertising can lure consumers to market and dramatize a product. But once a consumer arrives at the store, he's no longer a captive of the ads that brought him in. Ad recall doesn't necessarily equal sales. He may react more favorably to another product because its visual presentation has more integrity. That's the edge you must create.

Freshly-baked bread—French, Italian-style and particularly sourdough—is a tradition in San Francisco, with a long history stretching back to the gold strike at Sutter's Mill in 1849. So it seems right that our very first food packaging assignment was for the bakery founded by immigrant Isidore Boudin in that year. In our search for the right visual style, we eventually updated the wrapper—all the way to 1890s Victoriana.

Designing packaging for a San Francisco bread is like painting a mural on city hall: Everybody notices. When the owners of the Boudin Bakery decided to open a retail bakery on famed Fisherman's Wharf, they asked us to create an identity for the bread and the stores. The result was something of a phenomenon.

TWELVE STORIES

Although Boudin is one of the oldest bakeries in the Bay Area, in 1974 it had a number of solid competitors. One of these, the Parisian brand, had a very strong shelf presence as its packaging had been designed by the late Marget Larsen, one of the city's best designers. Her use of red, white and blue from the French flag and minimalist graphics provided a captivating contrast to the soft, sensual bread loaves.

The families who owned Boudin Bakery, the Giraudos and the Rivas, had determined to open a retail shop on Fisherman's Wharf. They wanted a new look for their product, one that could also be used in the store.

At the beginning of the assignment, my thinking was very much influenced by what Marget Larsen had done for Parisian. But after visiting the bakery and talking with Steve and Lou Giraudo, I began to appreciate the passion and commitment the company had for its products.

They showed me packages the firm had used in the past and photographs stretching back into the last century. As they talked, I realized they were looking for a design that portrayed their long history and tradition.

Unlike the corporate identities I had been working on most recently, in which everything is reduced to its most essential elements, this situation seemed to call for an approach that was almost ornate in its style. I felt that if the trademark was complex and elaborate—hand illustrated—by association, consumers would pick up on the concept that the bread was a handmade product.

In looking at graphics from the turn of the century, I saw that the designs were often worked around a single letter. Starting with a capital "B" I began piling on lines and ornaments to recreate the Victorian style. I rendered two stalks of

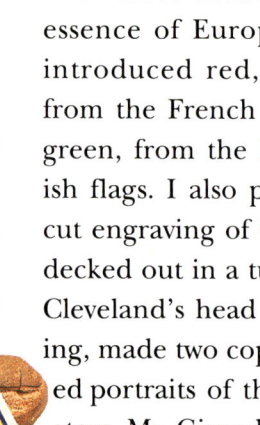

wheat to flank the letter and a long ribbon to carry the legend "Since 1849." To capture the essence of European tradition, I introduced red, white and blue from the French flag and a bit of green, from the Italian and Spanish flags. I also picked up a steel-cut engraving of Grover Cleveland decked out in a tuxedo. I removed Cleveland's head from the engraving, made two copies and substituted portraits of the current proprietors, Mr. Giraudo and Mr. Rivas.

The brand mark itself was complete, but as a package, it needed something more, something special. I created a newspaper-like format for the bags and sketched in type. The words included a history

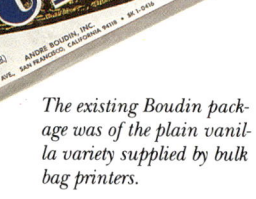

The existing Boudin package was of the plain vanilla variety supplied by bulk bag printers.

of bread making in San Francisco. Like a cereal box, they gave people something to look at, to read. One panel carried recipes from restaurants that served Boudin Bread.

The reaction to the package was overwhelming. The bakery's marketing staff used it and their own abilities to push the brand to the forefront of the Bay Area market. A poster based on the design was selected to hang in the Palace of the Legion of Honor in San Francisco and in the collections of the Cooper-Hewitt in New York and other design museums around the world. The bread bags themselves became quite popular

Since its release in 1974, the design has been adapted to a wide variety of packaging materials.

My initial reaction was to create a contemporary package to compete with the Parisian bread package. After studying Boudin's history, however, I realized they should use their long tradition as a selling point.

Thirteen years after the Boudin package was released, we began revisions on the packaging for Toscana bread.

with tourists and the design has been enlarged for use on tote bags that are sold in area gift shops.

Meanwhile, in the course of the decade from 1974 to 1984, the number of bread companies in San Francisco declined. In 1984, Boudin merged with the Parisian, Colombo and Toscana brands to form the San Francisco French Bread Company, owned and managed by the Giraudo family.

One consequence was a need to reposition Toscana within the newly-created multi-brand line. At that time Colombo had the largest market share of any French bread in the area and Toscana was number two. A brand owned by a competitor was number three. In 1987, the company asked us for a design that would increase sales of Toscana without cannibalizing the market share of Colombo. Under the circumstances, the approach used for Boudin was not viable. Toscana needed something to set it apart from Boudin and from the other brands in the corporate line.

Because it's owned by the same company that sells Boudin Bread, Toscana needed a package that would help it increase sales without cannibalizing the market share of its sister brands.

We used our graphics workstation to generate about two dozen variations for Toscana. Its flexibility allowed us to quickly try out color schemes and even take a look at translucent packaging materials.

The new packaging preserves Toscana's well-known logotype and familiar red-white-and-blue color scheme. These elements proved to be very important in retaining existing customers.

Although there are many similarities between the brands, our packages for Boudin and Toscana are very different; we couldn't just recreate the packaging done for Boudin in a different form. Boudin is sold in the bakery's own outlets or gourmet delicatessens while Toscana is a supermarket brand. Therefore, we felt its package should be bright and strong enough to project forcefully from among the welter of breads on the supermarkets' shelves.

How do you convince the top brass of an international company that it's time to update the firm's corporate identity? That was the challenge facing the U.S. executives of DHL Corp., the American arm of DHL Worldwide Express. It helps if you have aggressive managers in your corner. And when the company has principal officers in Hong Kong, it also helps to have the endorsement of a scholar expert in Chinese folk symbolism.

The year was 1982. DHL had virtually locked up the international overnight mail business. But in the U.S., DHL faced tough competition from Federal Express. That didn't seem to faze Charles Lynch, the new chief executive of DHL's North and South American divisions. Lynch planned to double sales within five years and capture a larger share of the lucrative U.S. domestic air express market.

Our involvement with DHL Corp. started with a phone call from John Beeby, who had recently joined the firm as marketing director. John realized DHL needed a more dynamic corporate identity to help position the company as a leader in the air courier business within the U.S. He envisioned a total identity program, starting with a redesign of the trademark. Unfortunately, some DHL executives in other international divisions had little enthusiasm for the idea.

"They weren't used to thinking in terms of corporate identity," John explained. "In their markets,

a corporate identity was little more than a trademark, and was rarely displayed prominently."

To get things started, John brought us in through the back door. The North American division had acquired its own fleet of jets, and they needed corporate markings. We got the assignment.

Knowing the resistance John faced from DHL's Hong Kong and London divisions we kept design changes to a minimum. DHL had a solid symbol with a great deal of equity, but visually, it had some excess baggage. It needed to be strengthened and applied consistently worldwide.

Our design team, which included myself, Ray Honda and John Lodge, explored a number of symbols before settling on a revised version of the existing DHL identity. The mark was applied to packaging to help visualize how it would look in use.

We kept DHL's color scheme, but used a more brilliant shade of maroon. We also changed the letters subtly. While we retained the block type to symbolize strength, we made the "D" more distinct and scored a line through the image. We also smoothed corners and condensed the letters to give them more height and velocity.

Steve Waller, DHL executive vice president, had the difficult task of presenting the design to officials in the other divisions. They were very concerned about the subtle meanings of the design elements and how they would be perceived, especially in China, where numerology and similar folk traditions are still very important.

There was only one way to convince them the identity was appropriate; we hired James Bravar, a college professor who is an expert in Chinese symbolism.

Getting the international divisions of the company to accept a change in corporate identity was difficult. Our hiring of a scholar of Chinese symbolism helped convince them that the visual elements—especially the line scored through the center of the design—were appropriate.

Bravar pointed out that the line through the image represented a strong *ch'i*, or life force, and that the letters were composed of six elements, a lucky number in Chinese folklore. With Bravar's analysis, all of the divisions gave their blessing. That was in 1986. Today, the new identity can be seen on DHL's fleet of aircraft and trucks, air bill forms, corporate literature and uniforms worldwide.

Our Chinese scholar helped make the final sale, but we would have never gotten that far without the vision of Charles Lynch, the determination of Steve Waller and the perseverance of John Crane, our senior vice president who helped turn a minor job into a worldwide identity program. Together, they convinced the decision makers at DHL that global dominance starts with a strong and consistent identity program.

Most packaging is destined for the hyper-competitive world of the retail shelf. Challenged by the need to make an impression in a fraction of a second, designers are caught between the clients' often conflicting desires for instant recognition and sophistication. The Shaklee Corporation sells its products through direct sales reps; there are no retail displays to consider. Creating packaging for Shaklee products was a delicious exercise in freedom.

Cable television shopping shows, catalogs and telephone solicitors have all but made door-to-door salesmen extinct. Armed with little more than their own audacity and a good pair of gum-soled shoes, these hardy souls made money the old fashioned way. With annual sales over $400 million, the Shaklee Corporation has proved that one-to-one salesmanship still works. Of course, the products are good. And we felt they should also *look* and *feel* good to consumers.

T W E L V E   S T O R I E S

Despite Shaklee Corporation's success with direct sales—or perhaps because of that success—it had never carefully considered the role of packaging in positioning its products to consumers. Unlike goods sold at retail, whenever Shaklee products are presented, a live salesperson is there to help focus the buyer's attention, answer questions about the product and persuade.

But the early 1980s were rough on the company. Women were a significant part of its direct sales force, and as more of them found jobs in traditional businesses, the Shaklee sales force dwindled and sales volume declined. As part of its commitment to rebuilding sales, Shaklee closely examined its marketing effort, including the way it packaged and presented products. We were asked to evaluate the packaging and suggest ways to make it work harder.

In this case, working harder didn't mean shouting louder.

The 1980s introduced a new kind of consumer, one interested not only in quality, value and price, but in esthetics as well. Customers knew Shaklee products

Shaklee's Classic line of cosmetics was intended to go head to head with the upscale department store brands. Our goal was to make them look like they belonged on an elegant vanity.

Without the neeed to compete at retail, we were able to develop an elegant image for Shaklee Naturals skin care products. The response from consumers and sales reps, many of them women, was positive.

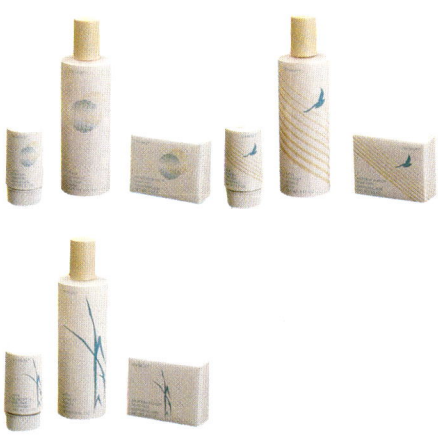

We tried a variety of approaches for the personal care products. To distinguish them from the Shaklee Naturals, we created a look that was pleasant, functional and very mainstream.

for their quality, but the packaging didn't quite live up to the product. This assignment exemplified the need for the realization that the package is the product and the product is the package. The two elements aren't separate because consumers see them as part of the larger experience they have with the product.

We began work on the Shaklee Slim Plan, a diet aid, in 1982. The company was selling Slim Plan as a carefully researched, almost clinical, diet supplement. However, the existing packaging, featuring photographs of food, was very busy. We gave it a more prestigious look by using a white background and gold foil seals. Subordinate lettering for the main product, a cocoa drink mix, was done in beige against a chocolate-brown band to add warmth and appetite appeal. Similar graphic treatments were developed for the instant soup and candy.

The new Slim Plan debuted in January 1983, and by September, Shaklee reported its field force had sold $65 million worth.

This success meant more than just money in the corporate treasury. Shaklee had been losing field reps as more women chose traditional business careers. The sales of Slim Plan were important because most of their new field reps are recruited from among their customers. New customers meant a new pool of potential sales reps.

The company's next move was the introduction of a line of natural skin and hair care products and a cosmetics line.

As with the Slim Plan, we weren't constrained by the need to

After the successful introduction of the Shaklee Classic cosmetics and Shaklee Naturals lines, the company asked us to design a series of fragrances—both men's and women's—as extensions to the line.

Although the fragrances weren't sold at retail, we styled them to compete visually with the "name" fragrances. We felt the customer would be more comfortable using and displaying the products if they were elegant and stylish.

compete on a retail shelf. Our goal, therefore, was to design products that would comfortably blend with the customers' home or office environments. We wanted them to feel good about leaving these products out on a bathroom counter, or on their desk at the office. Why waste effort to achieve high impact when we had the opportunity to really condition the package to fit esthetically in the consumer's environment?

We formulated a logo for the Shaklee Naturals line; a stylized "SN" in a loose script so that it looked a bit like a signature. The name "Shaklee" doesn't have the charisma, the kind of verbal euphony that some other cosmetics enjoy. Names such as Lancome,

Clinique and Estee Lauder were all carefully crafted to *sound* elegant. We made "SN" the focus of the package and moved the Shaklee name to a subordinate position on the label.

The Shaklee Naturals were made of all-natural ingredients so we wanted them to look clean and pure. We used a white background and found a soft, Wedgewood blue for the tops of the containers and the type. The boxes were also done in white with blue tops.

The look for the new Shaklee Classics cosmetics was a bit harder and brassier. These weren't all-natural products, but were intended to compete with upscale department store brands. Again, we developed a logo, this time a stylized "S" within a patch of bright maroon. The boxes were finished in high-gloss white and the tops echoed the maroon used behind the logo.

The introduction of these two lines, in 1984, went very well and we were asked to design a fragrance line—Lapis, Whispers, Metro and Zoe—in 1987. These were also visually positioned against mainstream fragrances, to draw sales from consumers accustomed to buying "designer" fragrances in department stores.

Sales of Shaklee's Slim Plan supplements totaled $65 million in the first nine months after the redesign.

We strive to make our packages fit the product. If we're working on a functional item we don't exaggerate it by designing an overly sophisticated package. But if the product is exceptional in some way, that should be shown. If the packaging promises too much *or* too little, buyers will see the inconsistency and the package won't be believable.

It reads like a story out of Fortune: In an abandoned warehouse in Lodi, California, two boyhood pals brew up a concoction of fresh fruit, juice, Chablis and a splash of carbonated water, pour it into bottles, affix a homespun-style label and become millionaires virtually overnight. Then along come two guys named Bartles & Jaymes, wisecracking television detective/actor Bruce Willis and a slew of market-wise competitors.

It's a safe bet you'd never catch Philip Marlowe or Sam Spade sipping anything less potent than three fingers of whiskey, neat. When they were America's toughest gumshoes, real men drank rye: Bushmills when they could afford it, Old Overholt if they were between cases. But that was the 1940s. In the 1980s, the watchwords are sweet, light and less intoxicating. Even tough-talking detectives prefer Beaujolais to Bourbon. And naturally, it all started in California.

T W E L V E S T O R I E S

Heading into the 1980s, consumers were thirsty for sweet, low-alcohol libations, as two entrepreneurs proved in 1981 when they introduced California Cooler, a blend of Chablis wine and fresh fruit juice with a dash of carbonated water. In their first year, Stu Bewley and Mike Crete sold 700 cases of the trendy potion. The two boyhood chums created a big splash virtually overnight and soon found themselves controlling 100 percent of a product category headed for $1 billion in sales.

By 1985, Bewley and Crete were shipping over 10 million cases of California Cooler annually and posting sales of $285 million. Not bad for a company founded in an abandoned warehouse.

Meanwhile, in the well-appointed offices of E&J Gallo Winery, Seagram & Sons, Strohs *et al*, executives had been watching with intense interest as California Cooler created an entirely new beverage category. Naturally, it wasn't long before California Cooler was sharing precious shelf space with Seagram's wine cooler, Gallo's Bartles & Jaymes and scores of other regional and national brands. By the end of 1986, although its sales were still rising, California Cooler's share had plummeted to 22 percent of the category it had pioneered.

With the beverage giants knocking at their door, Bewley and Crete decided to sell their company to Brown-Forman Corporation, the Louisville distiller. Brown-Forman had the right stuff to go toe-to-toe with Gallo and Seagram: Well-established distribution channels and, equally important, the

There was a great deal of equity in the original logo that the new owners, Brown-Forman, wanted to retain in the redesign.

Three variations on a theme: clear bottles that show different flavors (left), product label separated from neck band (center) and color-coded labels on green bottles, none of which were used.

resources to match Gallo dollar for dollar in what had become a game with very high stakes indeed: In 1986, the five leading wine coolers spent $110 million for advertising.

Despite having put up a reported $146 million to buy California Cooler, to its credit Brown-Forman didn't leap into the fray precipitously. It started by reorganizing its corporate sales force to give the brand more muscle at the wholesale level. There was one other challenge facing the new owners: California Cooler needed a much stronger shelf presence if it was to regain the lead position.

Brown-Forman, called us in April 1987 about designing a packaging system that could be extended to new flavors of California Cooler. Focus groups were to be conducted in San Francisco at the end of the month, and it was suggested that we attend to learn more about the wine cooler market and cooler consumers.

Although we often begin an assignment with the marketing goals already established, executives at Brown-Forman were still searching for the most powerful repositioning strategy when we got involved. Some felt that the product should look less like an alcoholic soft drink and more like a sophisticated wine product.

When the stakes are very high, disagreements over positioning

 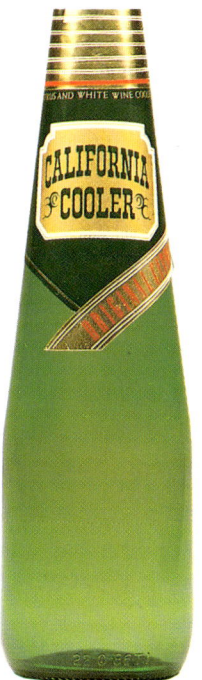 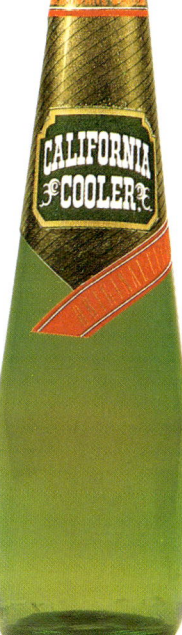

Given the fact that the product would most often be displayed in a carrier pack, we developed a neckband style label and positioned it near the top of the bottle.

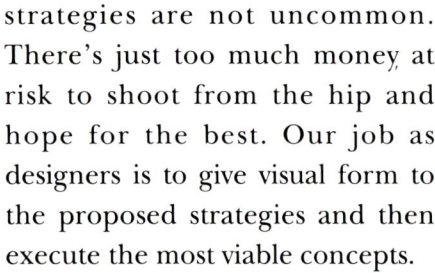

Premium Dry was a new product intended to appeal to consumers' desires for a dry—as opposed to sweet—wine cooler.

strategies are not uncommon. There's just too much money at risk to shoot from the hip and hope for the best. Our job as designers is to give visual form to the proposed strategies and then execute the most viable concepts.

We worked up color comps on more than thirty designs covering a wide range of styles and color schemes. The existing California Cooler label typified the brand's humble beginnings. The Western-style logo hinted at tradition, but lacked the finesse and believability of a well-integrated package.

Some of the comps incorporated a slightly refined version of the original brand mark, while others took a completely different tack. At this stage, you've got to design with the attitude that anything goes. Of course, you know in the back of your mind that the client will feel some of the designs aren't appropriate. But it's important to experiment freely because that freedom may lead you to create a more appropriate design, or at least to produce a look that stimulates productive discussions.

Fortunately, we were working with a very open-minded team. As you're refining marketing objectives, it helps if everyone involved can critique an idea objectively. Great ideas come from openness toward change and willingness to keep looking for a better solution. Adjustments are part of the process. It doesn't make good business sense to stubbornly hang onto a particular design that, whatever its attributes, clearly isn't the best solution.

The hard work paid off. By July we had an extensive list of design strategies for Vickie Cero, our

Creating a billboarding effect on the retail shelf is an essential design requirement. When massed together, products make a powerful statement to consumers.

embattled project director.

The list covered every aspect of the package. Every detail was considered, including what the neck band would look like after the cap was removed.

Our new bottle design became the cornerstone of the package. It presents a more elegant image than the old bottle, which was more appropriate for a beer. The bottle is topped by a gold foil cap and seal, which give the appearance of sophistication, and highlight the new logo—a cleaner version of the existing brand identity. The original typeface was too ornamental; it made the product appear too "sweet."

The bright metal accents set off the colors used to distinguish the new California Cooler flavors —Premium Orange Splash, Premium Tropical Berries and Premium Peach— and also worked very well with

Four-pack carriers were part of the new packaging scheme. Graphics of fresh fruit and a simplified range of colors help the packs project a strong image on the retail shelf.

the green label of the flagship variety, Premium Citrus.

The colors of the labels for the new varieties had to be distinct enough to call attention to each, but similar enough that both individual bottles and the four-pack carriers would blend easily to create a billboard effect when stacked together on a retail shelf. For added taste appeal, we included brilliant graphics of fresh fruit on the four-pack carriers.

We added the phrase "The Original" to the cap to remind people that California Cooler was the first wine cooler. There was some discussion as to whether it should simply say "original." Our feeling was that this wasn't just an original product, but *the* original wine cooler. Since no competing company could make this claim, we felt it should be highlighted.

It's essential for the design team to get involved very early in the

marketing process. Brown-Forman brought us in at the right time—while their strategies were still being formulated—and gave us the time and the resources to follow the project through to a successful conclusion. They were very aware of the need for creative interaction with the designers, giving enough time at each stage for everyone to reflect on the designs, evaluate each with a clear eye, and then move on to the next level.

Collectively, the myriad of small finishing touches added during the course of the project succeeded in creating a more believable image while retaining the brand's equity.

Beverage markets are hotly contested by strong, international marketing companies. That makes beverages difficult, but exciting, products to design. Good designs flow from a good design process: The design team and the client must be very specific in how they communicate to make sure that good ideas don't fall through the cracks because they aren't presented well enough. Great ideas and great designs can come from effective interaction.

The more advanced packaging technology becomes, the less edible it looks and feels to the consumer. The unfamiliarity with laminated foil, aseptic boxes and barrier pouches all combine to baffle the senses. While shoppers have generally been quick to embrace the advantages of new packaging, their minds still long for sensations: The bright colors of fresh fruit, the aroma of fresh-brewed coffee. Whatever its technical qualities, projecting sensations is the single most important task of any package.

Capri Sun was already a major success in Europe when the rights to market the fruit drink in the U.S. were acquired by Shasta Beverage Company in 1979. The drink was unique in that it was the first American beverage packaged in a foil pouch. In addition to selling the new brand, Shasta faced the challenge of selling juices in soft, opaque pouches to consumers accustomed to see-through glass bottles.

TWELVE STORIES

A wise man once noted that there are better things to do than that for which the world is not yet ready. In 1979, however, aseptic packaging, which can keep perishable foods fresh without refrigeration, was an idea whose time had clearly arrived.

That was the year the Shasta Beverage Company obtained the rights to market a unique aseptic pack fruit drink in the U.S. The beverage had been sold very successfully in Europe by a German firm under the name *Capri Sonna* (Capri Sun). The package, a triple-laminated aseptic film and foil pouch, was unique because it was soft and flexible, yet it could stand upright quite easily. It was sold with a straw, which consumers could use to puncture a weak spot on the pouch and sip the contents. The pouches packed easily, were convenient—no spills, no broken glass—and didn't need to be refrigerated, making them ideal for a child's school lunch box, among other things.

The only real hurdle was that American consumers weren't used to foil pouches. They were used to buying juice in glass jars, where the brilliant fruit color of the juice contributes greatly to appetite appeal. Knowing they would be substituting shiny foil for appetizing clear glass, Shasta asked us to create a packaging system for the new line.

My first thought was that the foil pack was a beautiful thing to start with. The structure was very attractive and it had sold well in Europe. Our one concern was that its appearance was too high-tech; by itself, it didn't project the kind of wholesome, natural feeling needed to sell a fruit juice.

We decided to experiment with an ornate graphic treatment as a counterbalance. Shasta had decided to call their product "Pockit," and we began our rough designs

While we were working on the roll-out of Capri Sun, Shasta also moved to stake out a position in the juice-added soft drink category. We created a similar, but clearly different, design for the soda varieties (below).

with the intention of illustrating the use of the foil pouch right on the label. We were trying to achieve a style reminiscent of orange crate labels of the 1920s by using highly stylized type with a big, realistic illustration.

There was one final alteration before the products went into the test markets—Shasta's German partner suggested we change the name to Capri Sun, which had worked so well in Europe.

In preliminary tests, the product achieved extraordinarily high purchase rates for a new beverage.

Meanwhile, we had changed the lettering to read "Capri Sun" and refined the graphics. The presses rolled and Capri Sun rapidly became the number one brand in its category.

For a package to be believable, the design must express some aspect of the product's personality. You can design something that looks terrific, but if it doesn't have that connection, consumers may well say, "I don't believe that, it's superficial." Consider the illusion of texture you're creating and express the product's personality; otherwise the product will become generic and fail to project from the shelf.

An imposing edifice does not make a museum great; only worthy collections can do that. But it seems a museum must have a great temple in order to be taken seriously. When Avery Brundage left his vast collection of Asian art to the city of San Francisco, the only place it could be housed was in a wing of the de Young Museum. The Asian Art Museum needed a strong identity to boost attendance and make potential donors aware of the richness of its collection.

Creating a complete identity system is always more complex—if not more difficult—than designing a single brand mark. Often, the identity has to work on an array of materials ranging from fund-raising solicitations to restroom signage. This assignment had the added challenge of reflecting the cultural diversity of an entire continent, with all that implies for color choices and symbolism.

TWELVE STORIES

Our first group of exploratory designs were abstract symbols, many of them circles, which could be combined with a literal logotype. As we worked through them, we felt there was a more unique way of solving the problem.

When philanthropist and businessman Avery Brundage donated his collection of Asian art to the city of San Francisco in 1966, the only condition of his gift was that the city provide a space to house and display the works. The Brundage collection is arguably the finest assemblage of historic and contemporary Asian art in the Western world. The Asian Art Museum was formed to curate the collection, but ironically, the only space the city could give it was in one of the wings of the M.H. de Young Memorial Museum in Golden Gate Park.

The public's impression of most museums is derived at least in part from the size and impact of the buildings that house them: The Guggenheim Museum on Fifth Avenue in New York, designed by Frank Lloyd Wright, is one of the most recognized buildings in the world. Without a physical edifice to speak for it, the Asian Art Museum needed a symbolic edifice, a vigorous and unique visual identity to assist the staff in raising funds for the museum and raising public awareness of the richness of the collection.

As the abstract symbols took shape, we were aware that some of them used symbolism appropriate to Japanese culture, others symbols appropriate to Chinese culture. We kept searching for a way to unify all of the varied cultures of Asia under one visual umbrella.

The final solution was to merge the symbol with the logotype. The eye first reads the block containing the word "Asia," and then recognizes the "N," so the mark reads both "Asia" and "Asian." To us, that nicely expressed the Asian philosophy that the spirit of the whole is contained within each individual.

The identity lends itself to a variety of uses, giving the museum staff a wide range of colors and forms to work with.

Our solution would have to work not only for promotional materials, but for stationery and for environmental graphics and informational signage within the Museum as well. The Museum had been using a rhinoceros as a sort of trademark. The rhino, a ceremonial vessel dating to the eleventh century B.C., was the rarest piece in the collection and had been the personal favorite of Mr. Brundage. Aside from being confusing, suggesting a zoo rather than an art museum, the piece was also identifiably Chinese. Yet the Museum contained art from all five Asian geo-cultural areas, and it was important that its identity mark not give preference to one region over another.

With Rand Castile, the Museum director and the chief curator, Clarence Shangraw, we generated a list of word pictures to characterize Asia. Our project director, John Cabot Lodge, began working with our designers to create an abstract symbol, one broad enough to encompass all of the Asian cultures.

In the course of the design exploration, some significant configurations began to emerge. We saw the word "Asia" inside a block with the letter "n" appearing just outside the block. The symbol and the logotype had merged, had become one element as well as two. This unique combination seemed to symbolically and literally express "Asia" and "Asian" as one. It became monolithic, projecting the necessary weight and gravity, but at the same time, it was right for a contemporary American—not Asian—audience.

The color choice was critical because of the great sensitivity of Asian cultures to the symbolism of

Sample applications were generated on our graphics work stations to show how the symbol could be used.

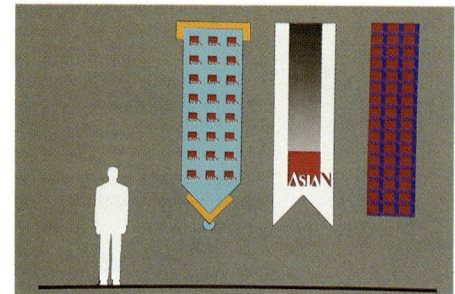

Flexibility of use was essential to the museum's environmental and signage needs.

color. Black was out as it is associated with death in certain cultures. Saffron, while very rich, is associated with Buddhism, which would exclude Moslems and people of other religions. We settled on cinnabar. Basically red, it also has some negative associations, but most of its associations are positive. The cinnabar-and-gray color scheme was conceived only as a starting point. The identity was embodied in the *form* of the symbol rather than in these specific colors, which allowed great flexibility for using the symbol in a variety of media.

This identity system is a little different, a bit more extravagant in its use of space than is usual. At first glance, the eye sees the word "Asia" with a "V" at the edge of it. On second look, it becomes "Asian." The time lapse of recognition has to be short, or the audience will get lost. Done well, this effect gives the mark a certain eccentricity that, hopefully, will keep it fresh and vigorous.

Making food products visually delectable is one thing, but how do you handle a food substitute? That was the question we faced in designing new packaging for the Cambridge Plan, a line of meal replacements created by well-known dietary researcher Dr. Alan Howard of Cambridge University. The answer: Luscious photographs of fruit to make the boxes into "kitchen art" which looks good enough to eat.

Let's face it. The truly awful thing about dieting is not eating. Passing up a second helping of Shrimp Scampi is painful but possible. But passing up a first helping would test the mettle of a monk. Not all of the satisfaction of Scampi comes through the palate, though. We also eat with our eyes. To help dieters stay with the Cambridge Plan products, we worked hard to make them sizzle visually.

TWELVE STORIES

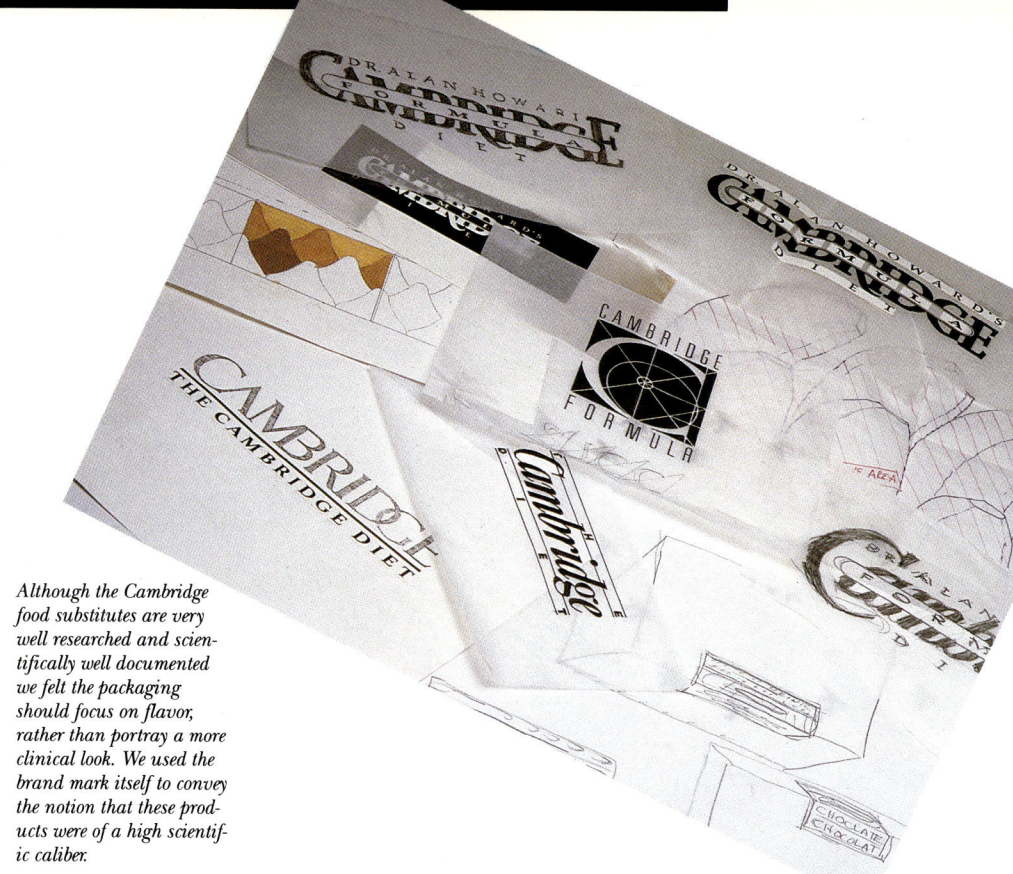

*P*erseverance is as important in design as in any other business. Dr. Alan Howard has it. After his Cambridge diet plan was released in the U.S., media reports inaccurately attributed a dieter's death to the product. Although the report wasn't true, the damage had already been done. Far from being the dangerous fad the newspapers portrayed, the Cambridge products are the culmination of nearly two decades of nutritional research conducted by Howard and others at England's Cambridge University. They aren't even available over the counter, being available only through trained diet counselors.

Although the rumors had crippled Cambridge Plan International, which sells the products in the U.S. market, Dr. Howard was determined to introduce his plan in Canada. After passing the stringent scrutiny of the Canadian health authorities, it was released there in 1985. A temporary black-and-white package was created so that the product could be shipped while we designed a permanent packaging system that would suit the company's marketing goals.

Although the Cambridge food substitutes are very well researched and scientifically well documented we felt the packaging should focus on flavor, rather than portray a more clinical look. We used the brand mark itself to convey the notion that these products were of a high scientific caliber.

Because the products aren't sold at retail, our strategy didn't need to include a highly-competitive package calculated to stand out on a crowded shelf, although our finished package does just that.

We started by trying to maximize the taste appeal. If dieters couldn't have the taste, texture and aroma of real food, they could at least have its familiar forms and bright colors.

The design brief called for packages for the strawberry, banana and chocolate flavors. The strawberries seemed to lend themselves to regimentation, lined up row upon row in a sparkling display. We quickly found a photograph that worked very well.

The first package for Cambridge in Canada was this black-and-white version, produced quickly to get them to market.

The banana and chocolate packages proved more difficult. From a distance, bananas look smooth and uniform. But up close, the skins of most bananas are mottled with patches of rust and green. Often, their surfaces are pitted by dry spots. If you think bananas go bad quickly on a kitchen window sill, try putting them under photographic lights. Day after day, Ming Louie, our photographer, picked up bananas fresh off the boat at the produce market early in the morning. Working quickly, he shot them, bunch after bunch, discarding the bunches as they dried under the hot lights.

Weeks of effort paid off in a shot that matched the strawberries for pure delectability.

After experimenting with chunks and blocks of milk chocolate, we decided that Hershey Kisses, those little brown pyramids of creamy pleasure, offered the most effective way to portray chocolate goodness.

Kisses are pointed at the top, and the points created a picket-fence effect when photographed side by side. We softened the ends of the Kisses by pouring molten chocolate over them and cooling them, creating a more rounded shape for our photo.

As Mark Twain once said about writing, "The difference between the right word and the almost right word is the difference between lightning and a lightning bug." Finishing the job for a client often means getting precisely the right photograph rather than a close approximation.

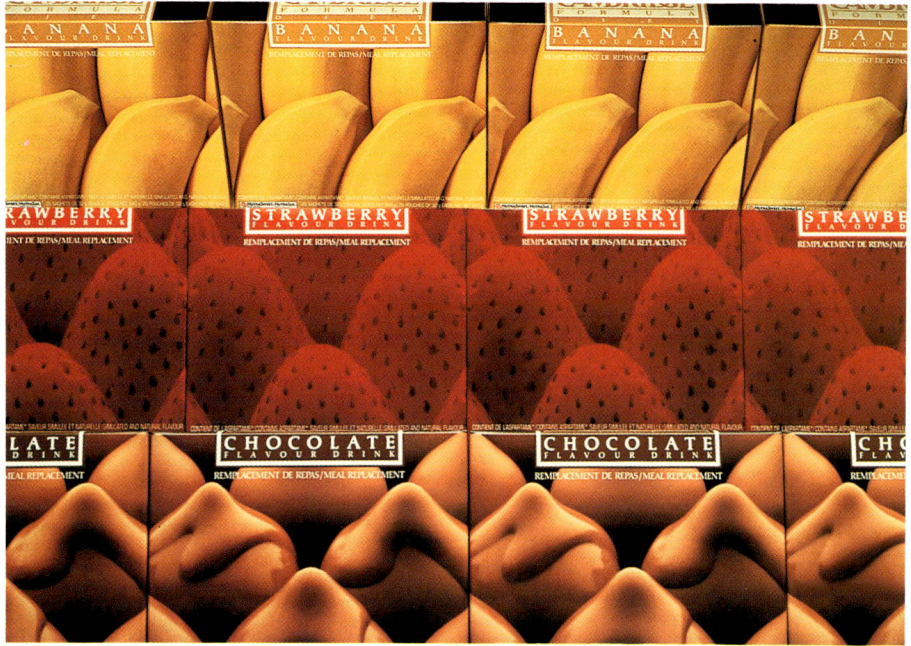

If massed together in a retail display, these boxes for the banana flavor product would create a powerful statement. Even in ones and twos, they create a tasty illusion.

We worked up a brand identity that highlighted the word "Cambridge" and found a way to incorporate a great deal of copy about the plan. To enhance the plan's credibility, we added a seal of approval featuring Dr. Howard's name and signature prominently.

With some work, these elements came together seamlessly, resulting in a well-integrated package.

The net result of the effort was that the introduction in Canada was very successful. It helped confirm our feeling that, for a diet product to be effective, it has to be used. By creating a package attractive and compelling enough to be left out in the open—on a desk at the office or a kitchen counter—we felt we were encouraging purchasers to use the product regularly. If they couldn't have all of the sensual satisfactions of a plate of chocolate, the photos would at least stimulate their senses visually.

Ironically—and happily—although we did not consciously strive for a look that would compete strongly in a supermarket, the final package is strong enough to visually hold its own in any environment. The key to this success is that the photographs are so literal. They project purity, the pure, undiluted flavor of fruit and chocolate.

GALLERY

Castle & Cooke created this beer in its brewery in San Pedro Sula, Honduras in 1982. The product would be imported to the U.S. in refrigerated ships. Our assignment was to name the product and give it a distinctive look that would portray its premium quality, Caribbean origin and method of transport.

When the goal is to sell a pricey product to a discriminating audience—such as gourmet chocolate lovers—the package must exude quality. Our approach was to use saturated colors and a style that would say "rich" and "elegant." The "ambassadorial stripe," a diagonal burgundy banner surprinted with gold lettering, immediately catches the attention of shoppers. Effective packaging doesn't stop with the outer surfaces of a container: Inside, a silver foil seal bears the Tres Chocolat logo.

We were asked to use Charles Shulz's Snoopy cartoon figure as the foundation for a sophisticated retail image that would appeal to both children and adults. Snoopy's doghouse, used often in Shulz's comic strip, was transformed into a take-out package.

Fono's is a San Francisco retailer of fine Italian gelatto. We created a complete identity for use as environmental graphics in the chain's shops and on take-out items.

When Carnation entered the rapidly-expanding ice cream novelty segment, they asked us to develop names and packaging for their products. They wanted a positioning that would appeal to all age groups—not just children or upscale adults—and to highlight the products' individual features. We used large-as-life product illustrations to give immediate appetite appeal. The format of the packaging is consistent to unify the line, while the colors are keyed to product varieties.

TWELVE STORIES

Thomas Cooper & Sons of Leabrook, Australia, produces ale using a 600-year-old brewing method developed in Oxford, England. Research revealed that U.S. consumers really liked the product but really disliked the label, which prominently featured a koala bear. Gold foil and block lettering impart the feel of an English pub sign, while the koala bear–now embossed on the bottle neck–promotes the brew's Australian heritage.

It's hard being number two in a product category behind a heavyweight like Quaker Oats. Our goal was to build a new and richer identity for the broad line of oat products produced by National Oats Company of Cedar Rapids, Iowa. Traditional lettering retains the equity of the brand, while bold colors give the packages greater shelf presence and, most importantly, taste appeal.

Foster Farms supplies poultry and deli items to supermarkets. Select Servings was a new product for them; poultry entrees ready to slip into oven or microwave.

When we picked up the Molinari & Sons assignment in 1981, company president Peter Giorgi told me, "I'll make the salami, you make the art." I don't think he had limited edition art in mind, but that's what we delivered in the form of a tongue-in-cheek repackaging announcement. Seven hundred autographed and numbered metal cylinders, each containing a salami, were sent to select customers and friends. The package received accolades from the New York Package Designers Council and major art directors' clubs. It also received worldwide press coverage as a "designer salami."

San Francisco bakery Just Desserts had won wide acclaim for its desserts, sold in its bakeries and served in fine restaurants.

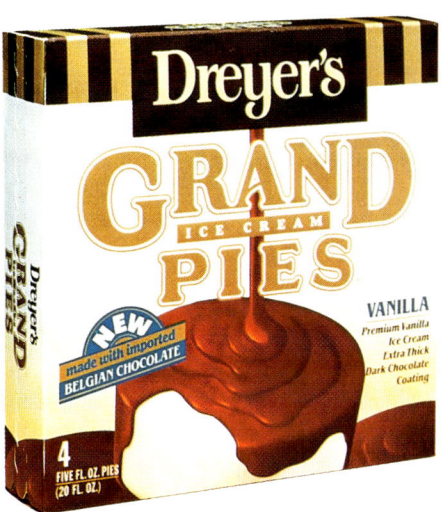

As Oakland-based Dreyer's Grand Ice Cream Co. prepared to enter selected Midwestern markets, they engaged us to find a brand name that was easy to pronounce and to create new, richer packaging for their ice cream pies.

When Shasta Beverage Company formulated its dLite line, they asked us to build a separate identity for their new diet soft drinks. The white background with fine vertical lines conveys the right impression of lightness.

The Shasta Beverage Company came to us in 1978 to update the Fifties-style graphics on its established brand of soft drinks. While finding the right attributes to portray on a soft drink container wasn't hard, devising a color scheme that could be extended to all 35 of the brand's flavors was.

Sunny Jim, a Northwest producer of quality food products, was losing market share. We were commissioned to create a stronger brand identity for the line of fruit products, peanut butter and pancake syrup.

Creating new packaging for Hills Bros. coffees presented several challenges. The brand, distributed in about half the U.S., is well-established. Understandably, the client was concerned about keeping the equity in their existing image. But they also needed to increase the brand's shelf impact and project a strong image that would justify its premium price.

PURE
Sunny Jim
SINCE 1921
"It's Good"
BLUEBERRY
PRESERVES
NET WT 18 OZ (1 LB 2 OZ) 510g

PURE
Sunny Jim
SINCE 1921
BLACKBERRY PRESERVES

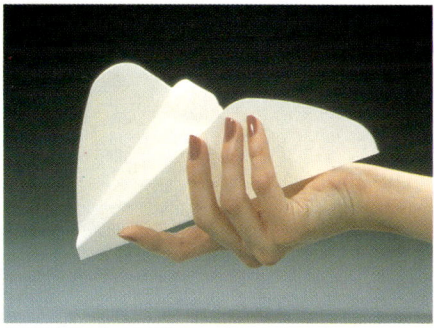

This product for women eliminates the need to sit on the seat of public toilets. The most amusing part of the assignment was coming up with a name.

When a manufacturer of natural cosmetics breaks into the mass market, it needs a stylized package design that's strong enough to compete with the likes of Procter & Gamble. The design scheme Mark Jones, Ray Honda and I devised for Jojoba Farms hair products and facial cream captured a Gold Award from the Package Designers Council in 1983.

Spray & Wipe

FORMULA 409

ALL PURPOSE CLEANER

NET 22 FL OZ
(1 PT 6 OZ) 651 ML

CAUTION: EYE IRRITANT. READ BACK CAREFULLY.

Even an established brand occasionally needs a face lift to revitalize its image. The Clorox Co. asked us to update Formula 409 cleaner to increase shelf impact and project a more contemporary image.

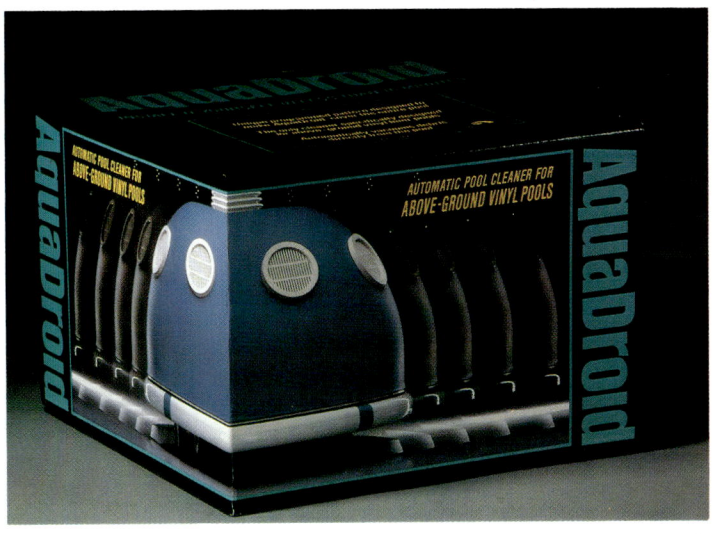

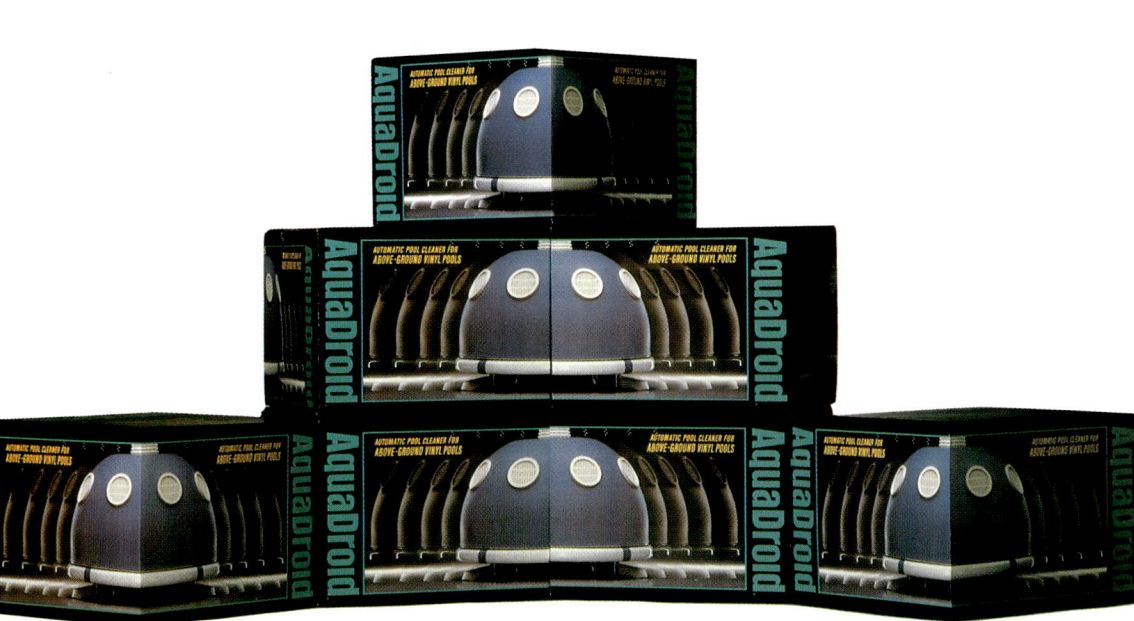

AquaDroid is an automated pool cleaner for above-ground pools. The large product illustration was used to immediately give consumers a look at the high-tech device. The offset outlines were intended to convey the idea of motion—AquaDroid moving around on the bottom of a pool. The illustration was wrapped around one corner of the box. Stacking the boxes in a mass display creates a billboard effect, with each box acting as one half of a double-size illustration.

Digital Research asked us to create an identity for their family of high-line computer products that would project sophistication and efficiency. Horizontal bands tie the line together and carry the product name. The smaller bands suggest the scanning lines of a computer display. Together with the silver-and-burgundy color scheme, they create a strong, consistent look.

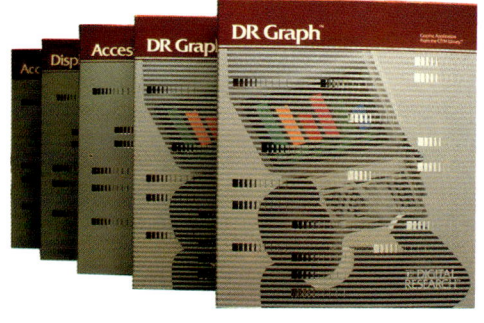

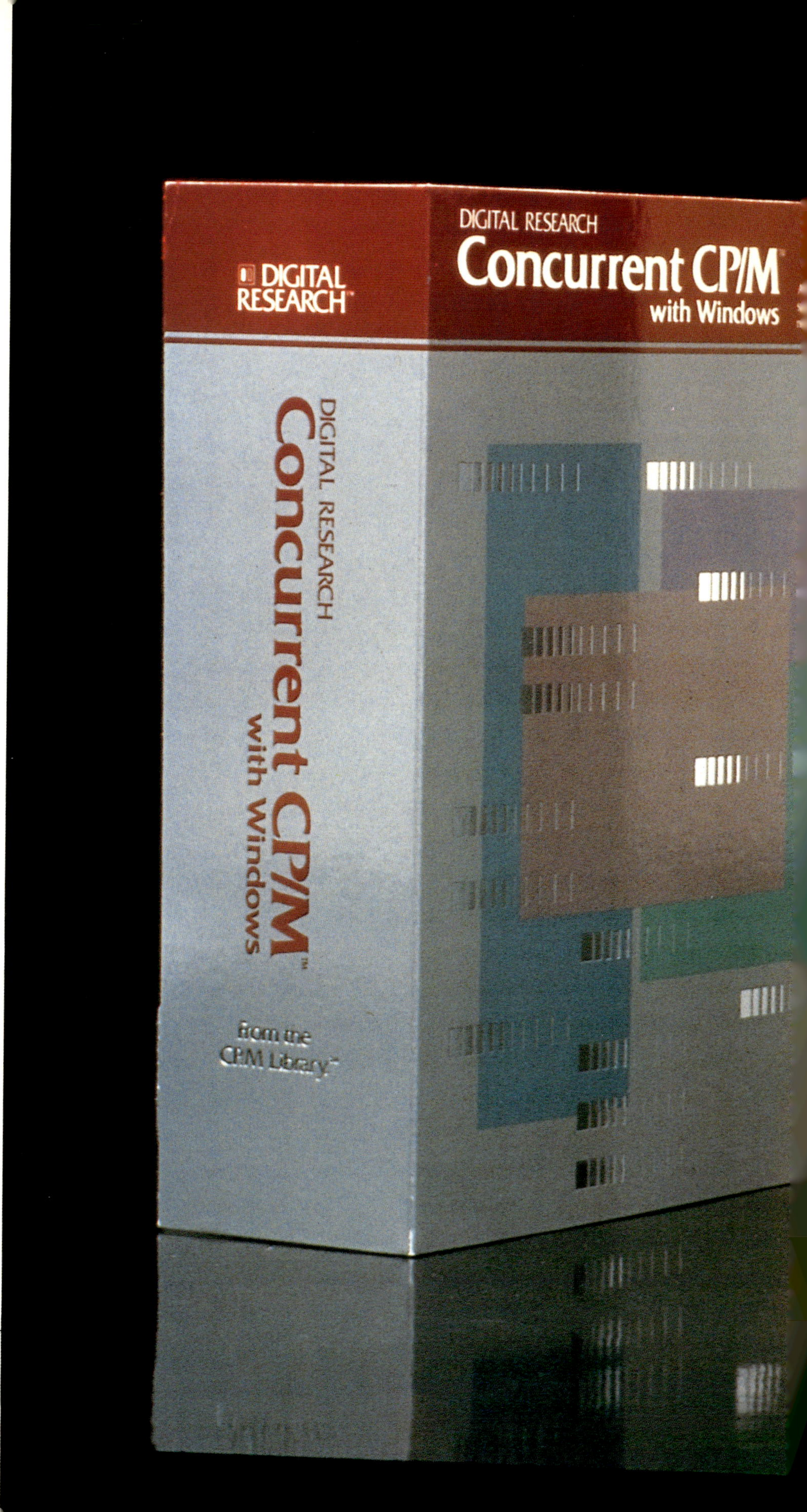

New uniforms for the Oakland Athletics play on the tradition of the Athletics ball club, the oldest team in the American League. The existing multicolor uniforms commissioned by former owner Charlie Finley—which looked like a show business costume—were replaced with a more traditional looking uniform featuring the Athletics logo and, on the sleeve, the symbol we created to commemorate the 1987 All Star Game played in Oakland. We used the letter A of the Athletics logo to form the revolving blue and red star.

This logo was created to commemorate the Giants baseball team's twenty-fifth year in San Francisco. The emblem was used as a shoulder patch on the player's uniforms, and for other items.

AMFAC operates hotels and restaurants in national parks, including the Grand Canyon Lodges. We were asked to design an identity program for some of their facilities. This design uses shapes from an American flag to suggest the contours and angles of the canyon's walls.

We adapted the existing Wells-Fargo Bank identity for use by its subsidiary, Wells-Fargo Credit Corp., utilizing the stagecoach and traditional lettering.

In designing a logo for the Western Art Directors Club, based in San Francisco, we used two hemispheres to suggest not only being in the Western U.S., but also being part of the Pacific Rim. The triangles form a highly-stylized W and A, while the hemispheres finish the initials of the organization.

A&W restaurants and soft drinks have been a part of the American landscape since 1922. In 1978, we were asked to enrich the chain's logo, which is also used on retail signage, food products and take-out items.

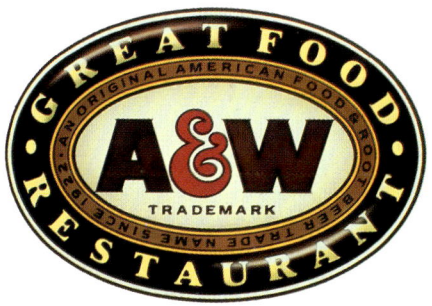

The 5,500-unit Pizza Hut chain decided to challenge the lunchtime dominance of the fast-food franchises by creating Pizza Hut Express; walk-in locations where customers can get a personal pan pizza in two minutes. We worked with an architect to build a retail environment that would feel "fast"—bright lights, white tile, vivid colors—and created this identity for the new chain.

Illumination Industries Inc. manufactures high-intensity light sources. The logo for the Silicon Valley concern is a highly-stylized representation of the inside of a lighting unit.

Logo for Barkow Petroleum, packagers and distributors of petroleum products.

Trademark developed for Learning Technologies, an Atlanta, Georgia-based producer of educational tools for teachers, appears on the company's wide assortment of products sold worldwide.

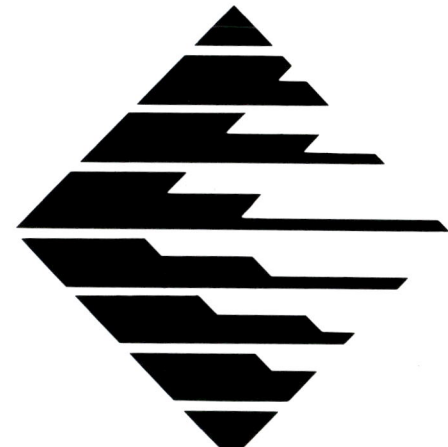

Trademark for Allied Medical Clinics, a national chain providing outpatient medical services.

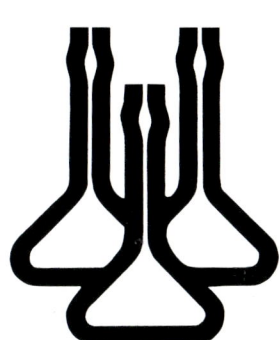

Biosciences Labs, Van Nuys, California, provides testing services for the medical field.

The original logo created in the early 1970s for AMFAC Marina Hotels symbolizes the hotels' waterfront locations.

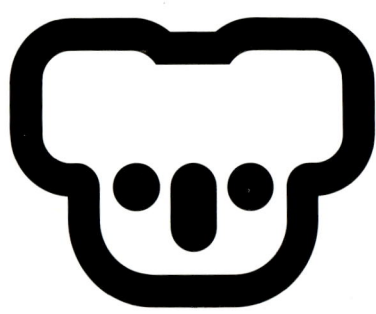

Koala Ware sells computer software for children that utilizes a touch-sensitive pointing device, the Koala Pad. Our packaging was rendered in bright colors with illustrations to intrigue children. A small graphic shows on each package shows that it is for use with the Koala Pad.

In 1983 Leisure Enterprises, a supplier of leisure equipment, found its name was inappropriate as the company had become the largest supplier of garden equipment in the U.S. Our identity program focused on the company's primary business.

GRiD

The Grid Compass was the first fully portable laptop computer. In 1983, we designed an identity for Grid and for the Compass, which packs an amazing amount of power into a case no larger than a notebook. Grid has become one of the thirty fastest-growing companies in the U.S., and the Compass is part of the permanent collection of the Museum of Modern Art in New York.

Vision Galleries is one of the foremost exhibitors of photography in California. They also offer extraordinary custom framing and ready-made frames.

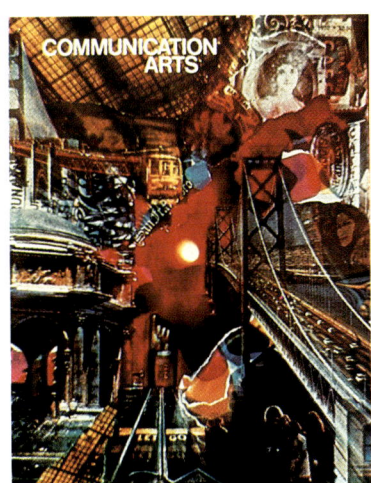

Dick Coyne, publisher of Communications Arts magazine, asked me to create a collage for the cover of the August 1984 issue. The piece was photographed by Lars Speyer.

Tommy's Joynt is a San Francisco institution. Crammed with Bay Area memorabilia, we gave the outside a wall mural that's almost as densely-packed as the eatery itself.

Another of our pro bono projects, Esthers Ironworks Cafe trains the physically handicapped to work in the food service business.

The Banana Republic clothing chain wanted a strong retail identity with an appropriate personality to tie together the private label and national brand items sold in its stores.

This book with slipcase was designed for a conference of franchisees of VISA International, the San Francisco-based credit corporation.

In America is a set of educational books designed to teach English to people who speak Japanese.

Vintage Properties is an ultra-exclusive development near Palm Springs, California. These promotional materials were intended to project exclusivity and luxury.

As a Christmas gift for clients and friends, this packaging was created for a book of logotypes of the 1920s and '30s, written by Eric Baker and Tyler Blik.

These architectural tiles are designed to be used as environmental graphics. Ranging in size from one square foot to two-by-two feet, they can be reorchestrated after installation, creating new combinations of shapes and colors.

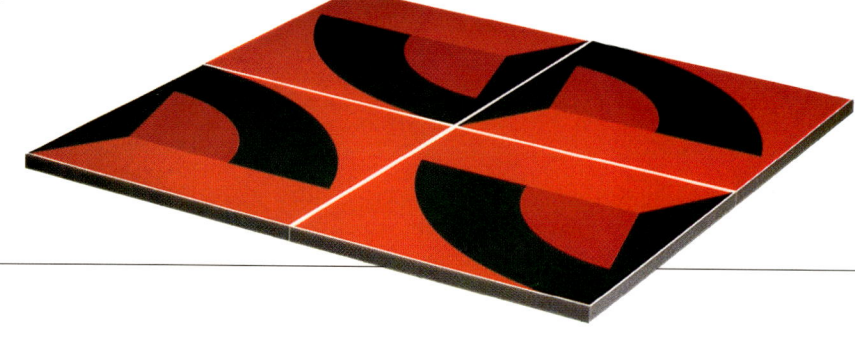

Another Christmas gift from our studio, this wrapping paper was created to give to clients and friends.

When Lorimar Telepictures went public, they asked us to design their first two annual reports. This spread highlighted one of their most creative films, Being There, which starred Shirley Maclaine and Peter Sellers. The 1983 report above highlighted Lorimar's Dallas television series and a motion picture feature to be released the following summer.

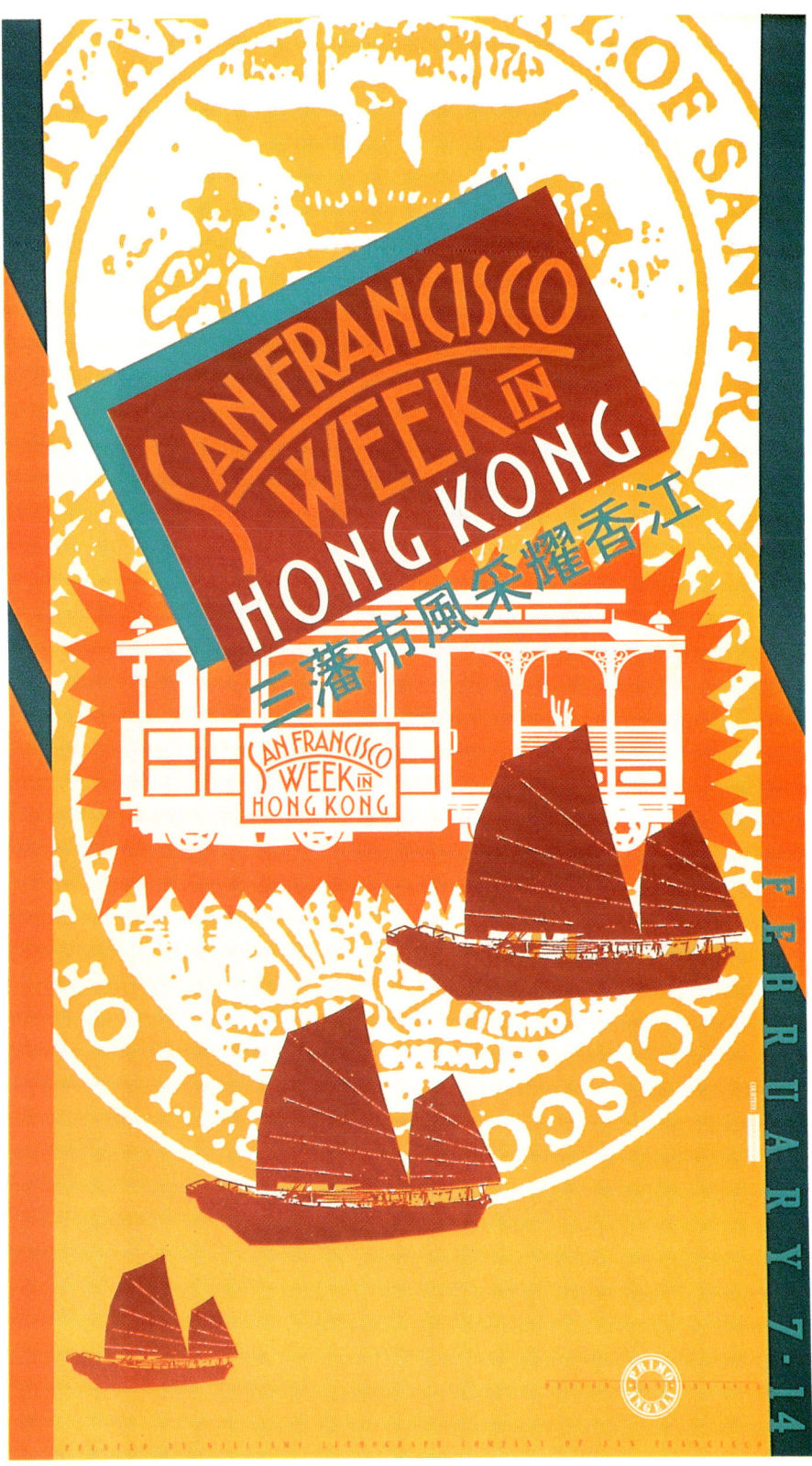

In February 1988, the city of Hong Kong invited San Francisco business leaders, the city's symphony, Mayor Diane Feinstein and city officials to a week-long celebration of our cities' long-standing friendship. I was a member of the delegation and created this poster to commemorate the event.

It was the early 1960s and the Broadway musical Hair was shocking the sensibilities of conservative Americans from coast to coast. This poster, with a photograph by Lars Speyer, was commissioned for the San Francisco opening of the show.

This poster was inspired by then-President Richard Nixon's phrase "silent majority." Photographer Lars Speyer and I created it in a day. The poster became very popular and is now part of the collection of the Museum of Modern Art in New York.

The posters (below and right) announce Festa Italiana, an extremely popular festival held every October at San Francisco's Pier 45. The four-day event attracts thousands of Italian Americans (and hundreds who wish they were). The poster for the first Festa, held in 1983, sports Italy's national colors and highlights the main attractions of the event—dance, drink, food and fun.

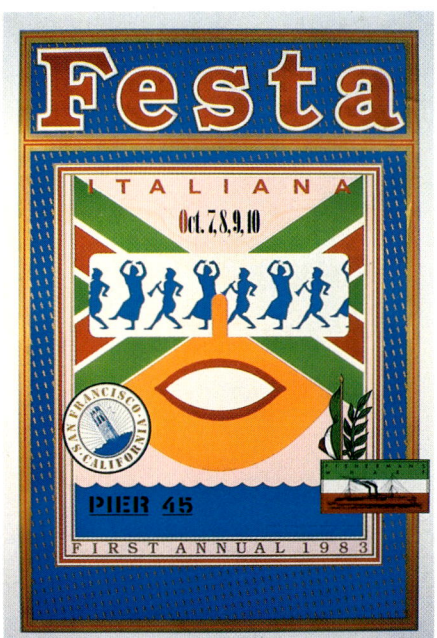

By 1985 Festa Italiana was attracting a broad cross-section of the Bay Area's population. We felt a more contemporary poster would boost the event's widening appeal, especially among youthful party goers.

When the San Francisco International Airport unveiled its new modern facilities in 1983, the city felt it was a good time to promote the airport's status as a major gateway to international destinations. The posters were mailed to business and civic leaders nationwide and were sold in airport gift stores. We also designed a press kit and other collateral material as part of the airport's identity package.

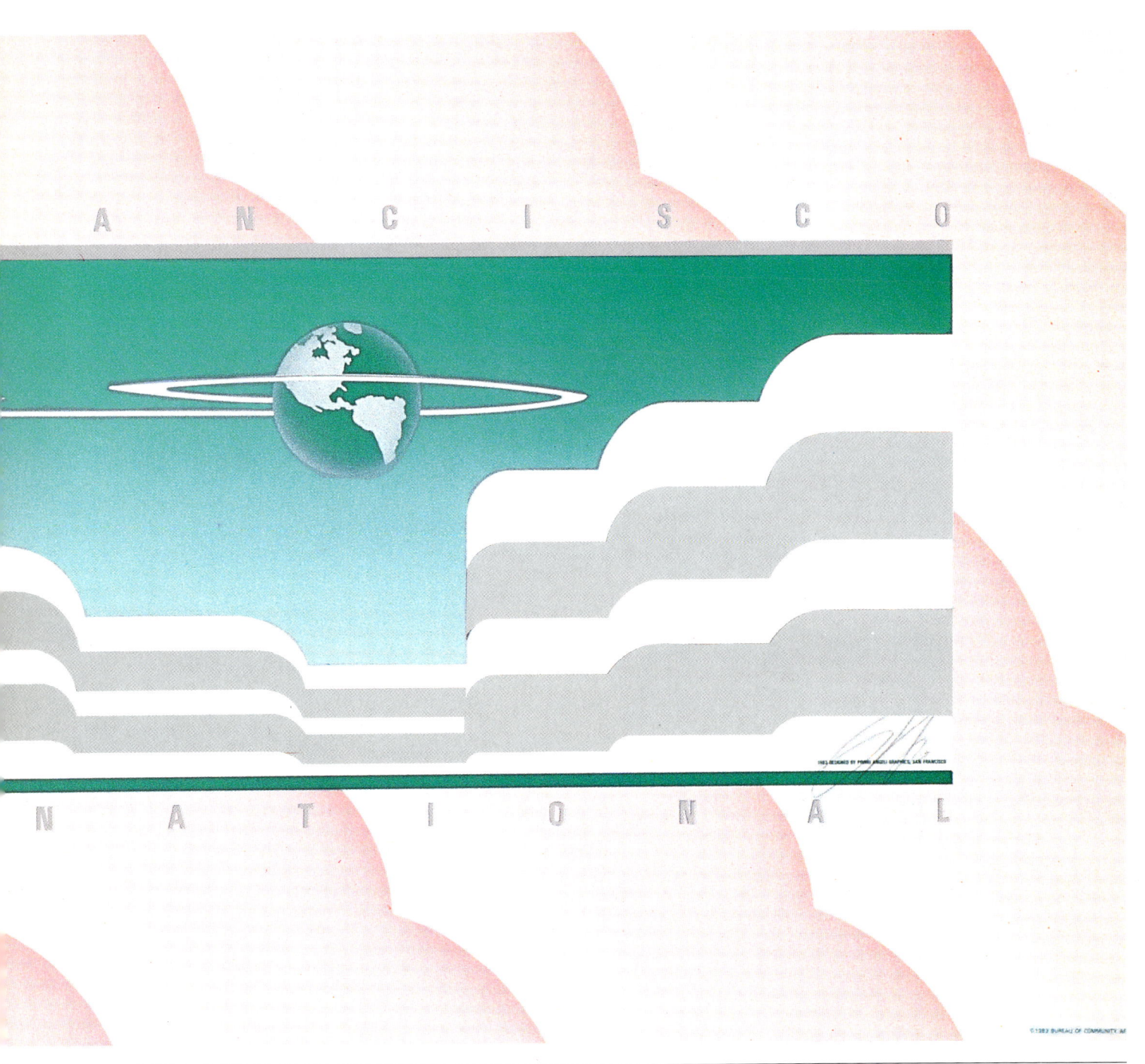

Every year the San Francisco Arts Festival brings together artisans, craftsmen and others from the city's large art community to exhibit their work. This poster was commissioned in 1983 by the Arts Commission of the City and County of San Francisco.

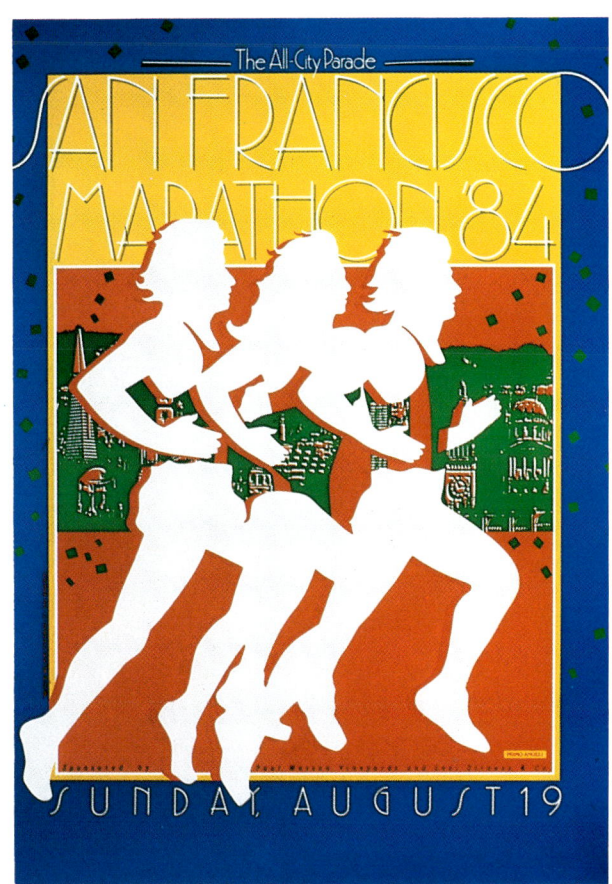

This poster promoted the 1984 San Francisco Marathon sponsored by Levi Strauss & Co. and Paul Masson Vineyards.

As a pro bono project, we designed a logo for the celebration of the fiftieth anniversary of the opening of the Golden Gate Bridge. The logo was used as an identity mark in all planning and promotion of the event. The Friends of the Golden Gate Bridge asked us to adapt the logo for use as a poster to commemorate the majestic structure and its new permanent lighting. We created an image that accentuates the bridge's Art Deco features and suggests illumination and celebration.

THE STUDIO

Primo Angeli Inc. offers a wide range of design and production services to its clients. The company occupied new space on Folsom Street in San Francisco in 1987. The interior was custom-designed to provide the designers with maximum access to support services and encourage free and easy personal exchanges. This helps further the PAI philosophy that the best designs are produced by talented communications professionals working as a team.

The designers' methods range from traditional techniques of carefully applying designs to composite packages by hand to quickly generating multiple iterations of a visual theme on the firm's graphic workstations.

AWARDS

In addition to receiving more than 250 awards—ranging from Clios and Andy awards from the New York Art Directors Club to medals from the Package Design Council and accolades from *Communication Arts* and *Graphis* magazines—Primo Angeli's designs have been made part of prominent permanent collections worldwide including those of the Museum of Modern Art in New York, Smithsonian Institutions in Washington, Cooper-Hewitt Museum in New York, Achenbach Collection at the Legion of Honor Museum in San Francisco, the Warsaw Poster Collection and the Centre Georges Pompidou in Paris.

INDEX

Allied Medical Clinics   115
AMFAC   110, 115
Anheuser-Busch   16-23
AquaDroid   105
Arts Commission, City and County of San Francisco   135
The Asian Art Museum   74-79
Awards   23, 95, 141
A&W Restaurants   111
Baker, Eric   124
Banana Republic   120
Barkow Petroleum   113
Barnhill, Steve   44
Beeby, John   54
Bewley, Stu   64
Biosciences Labs   115
Blik, Tyler   124
Blitz-Weinhard   16-23
Boudin Bread   18, 26, 46-50
Bravar, James   54, 55
Brown-Forman Corp.   64-69
Brundage, Avery   74, 76, 78
California Cooler   62-69
Cambridge Diet Formula   80-84
Capri Sun   70-73
Carnation   91
Castile, Rand   78
Castle & Cooke   86, 87
Cerlette, Larry   24
Cero, Vickie   66
Christian Brothers (The Brothers of the Christian Schools)   28-33
The Clorox Co.   104
Clio Awards   23
Communication Arts   9, 119
Conoco   42-45
Cooper-Hewitt Museum of Design   134
Coyne, Dick   9
Crane, John   55
Crete, Mike   64
M.H. de Young Memorial Museum   74, 76, 134
DHL Corp.   52-55
Digital Research   106, 107

dLite   99
Dreyer's Grand Ice Cream Co.   97
Dreyer's Grand Pies   97
Edy's Grand Pies   97
Esthers Ironworks Cafe   121
Ferrari, Paul   24, 26
Festa Italiana   130, 131
Friends of the Golden Gate Bridge   136
Fono's   91
Formula 409   104
Gallery   85-136
Garden America Corp.   117
Giorgi, Peter   95
Giraudo, Lou   48
Giraudo, Steve   48
Grand Canyon National Park Lodges   110
Grid Compass   118
Haas, J.D.   45
Hair (The Broadway Musical)   128
Henry Weinhard Beer   16-23
Hills Bros. coffee   100
Honda, Ray   32, 54, 103
Howard, Dr. Alan   80, 82, 84
In America   122
Illumination Industries Inc.   113
Jenkel-Davidson   129
Jojoba Farms   103
Jones, Mark   18, 32, 103
Just Desserts   96
Koala Ware   116
Lapis   61
Larsen, Marget   48
Learning Technologies   113
Le Funelle   102
Lodge, John Cabot   54, 78
Lorimar Telepictures   126
Louie, Ming   83
Lucca Delicatessens   24-27
Lynch, Charles   52, 55
Metro   61
Molinari & Sons   26, 95
Museum of Modern Art   129
Package Design Council   95, 103

Oakland Athletics   108, 109
Owens, Clint   34, 36-39
Palace of the Legion of Honor   134
Pizza Hut   111
Port Royal Export   86, 87
Posters   127-136
Quaker Oats   94
Riney, Hal   18, 21-23
San Francisco Arts Festival   135
San Francisco French Bread Company   50, 51
San Francisco Giants   110
San Francisco International Airport   132, 133
San Francisco Marathon '84   134
San Francisco Museum of Erotic Art   129
San Francisco Week in Hong Kong   127
Shaklee Corporation   56-61
Shaklee Classic   57-61
Shaklee Natural   57-61
Shaklee Slim Plan   59, 61
Shangraw, Clarence   78
Shasta Beverage Company   98, 99, 70-73
The Silent Majority   129
Snoopy's Original Ice Cream & Cookies   90
Speyer, Lars   128, 129
Starr, Kevin   10, 11
Strohs   64
Sunny Jim   101
Thomas Cooper & Sons   92, 93
Three Minute Brand   94
Tommy's Joynt   121
Toscana   50, 51
TreeSweet Products   34-41
Tres Chocolat   88, 89
Ultra Lucca   24-27
Vintage Properties   123
VISA International   122
Vision Galleries   119
Waller, Steve   54, 55
Wells Fargo Credit Corporation   110
Western Art Directors Club   23, 111
Whispers   61
Zoe   61